DIZZY SPELLS

THE KITCHEN WITCH BOOK 2

MORGANA BEST

By this act
And words of rhyme
Trouble not
These books of mine
With these words I now thee render
Candle burn and bad return
3 times stronger to its sender.
(Ancient Celtic)

GLOSSARY

The author has used Australian spelling in this series, so for example, *Mum* instead of the US spelling *Mom*, *neighbour* instead of the US spelling *neighbor*, *realise* instead of the US spelling *realize*. It is *Ms*, *Mr* and *Mrs* in Australia, not *Ms.*, *Mr.* and *Mrs.*; *cosy* and not *cozy; 1930s* not *1930's*; *offence* not *offense*; *centre* not *center*; *towards* not *toward*; *jewellery* not *jewelry*; *favour* not *favor*; *mould* not *mold*; *two storey house* not *two story house*; *practise* (verb) not *practice* (verb); *odour* not *odor*; *smelt* not *smelled*; *travelling* not *traveling; liquorice* not *licorice; leant* not *leaned; have concussion* not *have a concussion; anti clockwise* not *counterclockwise; go to hospital* not *go to the hospital; sceptic* not *skeptic; aluminium* not *aluminum; learnt* not *learned*. These are just some of the differences.

Please note that these are not mistakes or typos, but correct Aussie spelling and terms.

AUSTRALIAN SLANG AND TERMS

Big Smoke - a city

Blighter - infuriating or good-for-nothing person

Blimey - an expression of surprise

Blue - an argument

Bluestone - copper sulphate (copper sulfate in US spelling)

Bluo - a blue laundry additive, an optical brightener

Boot (car) - trunk (car)

Bonnet (car) - hood (car)

Bunging it on - faking something, pretending

Cark it - die

Come good - turn out okay

Copper, cop - police officer

Coot - silly or annoying person

Drongo - an idiot

Dunny - an outhouse, a toilet, often ramshackle

Fair crack of the whip - a request to be fair, reasonable, just

Flat out like a lizard drinking water - very busy

Galah - an idiot

Garbage - trash

G'day - Hello

Give a lift (to someone) - give a ride (to someone)

Goosebumps - goose pimples

Laundry (referring to the room) - laundry room

Like a stunned mullet - very surprised

Mad as a cut snake - either insane or very angry

Miles - while Australians have kilometres these days, it is common to use expressions such as, "The road stretched for miles," "It was miles away."

Mow (grass / lawn) - cut (grass / lawn)

Stone the crows! - an expression of surprise

Takeaway (food) - Take Out (food)

Torch - flashlight

Tuck in (to food) - to eat food hungrily

Ute /Utility - pickup truck

Vegemite - Australian food spread, thick, dark brown

Wardrobe - closet

Indigenous References

Bush tucker - food that occurs in the Australian bush

Koori - the original inhabitants/traditional custodians of the land of Australia in the part of NSW in which this book is set. *Murri* are the people just to the north. White European culture often uses the term, *Aboriginal people*.

CHAPTER 1

*T*hyme held two bags over her head. "You had better get in there, Amelia. Those sales won't last forever."

"I'm good, thanks." I smiled at my friend, who also happened to be my employee, as we left the store window and started down the busy footpath. The day was absolutely perfect for window-shopping, with a light breeze carrying along the scent of old English roses and gardenias from the local florist. All in all, it was a nice, pleasant shopping day.

"You need to get something to commemorate the occasion," Thyme insisted. "Your carrot cake was almost edible today. You'll be baking cakes before you know it."

I shook my head. "What do you mean? It was as

hard as a rock. Even the knife couldn't go through it. When I dropped it on the floor, it made a crack in the concrete."

Thyme beamed. "But you didn't set anything on fire!"

The trouble was, she was genuinely pleased about that. I'm not a good cook. In fact, it's a wonder that the government hadn't hired me to make me produce bio-hazardous waste with my baking. After all, I had sent my ex-boyfriend to the hospital with my nachos, and had been evicted from my apartment for the constant fires caused by my attempts at baking.

Yet by some strange twist of fate, I had been left a home and a cake shop by an aunt I had never met. I was expected to take my toxic waste and somehow make it edible enough to sell to customers. Real customers. It didn't help that a man had died during a cake tasting just after I arrived. I did have the consolation of knowing it wasn't the cakes that did him in, but I knew it would be a long day before cakes I myself had baked would be on display, unless it was in a museum of horrors. And ironically, being the owner of a cake shop was not the strangest thing that had happened to me since I arrived in Bayberry Creek.

"Hey, has that always been there?" I pointed to a sign I hadn't noticed before. The swirling, smoky lettering, along with golden stars painted in the centre, displayed the words, 'Madam Dianne's Shop of Mystery.'

"Oh, come on!" Thyme let out a frustrated whine and wrinkled her nose at the sign. "They leave this spot vacant for almost a decade, and they fill it with one of these jokers? They could have put in a health food shop. At least the herbs and special salts would have been useful."

I gazed into the window. "Is it that bad?" I at once jumped back when I came eye to eye with a skull. It took me a minute to notice the stump of a wick sticking out of its creepy painted face. There were stuffed crows along with several black roses scattered all over the display. I could also see books, crystals, glass displays full of jewellery, and various tarot cards.

"Very bad." Thyme sighed and shook her head. "These people are harmless, but some people take a touch of intuition and go way out there with it. They give our kind a bad reputation. As if Hollywood wasn't already doing a good enough job at that!"

"So this person isn't, well…?" My voice trailed

away. I was still trying to come to grips with the fact that magic existed, and with the fact that I was supposed to be practically overflowing with 'raw natural talent,' as Thyme put it at least once a week.

"The real deal?" Thyme asked, as she glanced around to see if anyone was in hearing range. "If she is, she doesn't know it. Take another look at her shop and tell me what you feel, compared to Ruprecht's shop."

I looked inside the shop again, bringing *Glinda's*, Ruprecht's books and antique store, to mind. It was like night and day, come to think of it. Where his shop was cluttered in a pleasant, lived-in way, this one screamed over-the-top and commercial with an artificial edge to it. Bright plush furniture and heavy velvet tablecloths with tacky stars, moons, and tassels were arranged everywhere. It was nothing like Ruprecht's homey, cozy shop at all.

"A mess," I said, earning a nod of acknowledgment.

"Excuse any clutter you see," a throaty, raspy voice crooned.

I jumped and turned from the window. A woman was trying to lounge alluringly on the garbage can right by the doorway. Her jet black curls screamed Halloween prop wig, and she was wearing layers upon layers of skirts to mimic a gypsy look, complete with a corset straining in its bindings around her ample belly. Her giant hoop earrings constantly bounced on her shoulders as she moved. I stared at the fire-engine-red lipstick and bright blue eye makeup. There seemed to be more eye makeup than actual eyes.

"We have traversed a great distance from our ancestral home to offer the guidance your spirit seeks," the woman said dramatically as she waved her hand before her.

"Thanks, but our spirits have GPS. No directions necessary," Thyme said with a giggle.

"Perhaps," the woman said thoughtfully, "you might be able to fool yourself. But the great Madam Dianne, she knows. The spirits whisper to me of your troubles."

I felt my stomach clench as I instinctively tucked my handbag under my arm. The woman looked nice enough. She was certainly eccentric, but nothing about her screamed that she was any sort of threat. Yet there was something about her theatrics that felt like slime had dripped down over me and soaked into my clothes. It was nothing like when I had met Ruprecht, Thyme, and the others.

"So how long have you been in town?" Thyme

said in a pleasant voice as she crossed her arms in front of her. "I didn't know anyone had moved in."

"I've only been here a short time," the woman said, seeming taken aback by the question. She did not seem prepared to give a dramatic answer this time. "Come in; come in. Madam Dianne shall tell you what the fates have in store for you!"

Thyme waved off the invitation. "Thanks, but I don't like spoilers. I like to keep life interesting. My friend and I have someplace to be anyway."

"Come now," Madam Dianne scolded in a gentle, encouraging tone, as if she were trying to reassure a young child. "There is no reason to fear the spirits. They are but messengers from worlds beyond. You need not fear the opinions of others over receiving a glimpse of your destiny. You have spirits right by your shoulder. Grandparents perhaps? They send you their love and blessings."

I tried to keep a straight face. Thyme was the opposite of fearful. She didn't concern herself with town opinion unless it had to do with the cakes.

I stiffened nervously as the woman trained her eyes on me. "The spirits also tell Madam Dianne that you should make peace with your mother. You need not work so hard for her approval. She'll come to understand that your life is your own, eventually.

Your spouse, though, you should keep an eye on. He keeps a dark secret from you."

"I'm not married," I blurted out, furrowing my brow at the randomness of the prediction. "And my mother passed away years ago."

The woman's eyes widened slightly. She gave a strained smile as she collected herself. "Ah, yes, yes. This I see. You and your partner do spend so much time together. A ring must be very close in your future. Sometimes the flow of time can be difficult to interpret."

"I'm sure," I said sceptically, suddenly over my initial nervousness. I was beginning to understand why Thyme was so unhappy to see the shop. If I had met this woman before Thyme's quiet little circle, I would have spent weeks trying to get past the idea that they were trying to scam me. Accepting magic had been difficult enough when they were acting normal, and that was even with my own house trapping unwelcome houseguests and spitting them out on the front yard.

The woman apparently mistook my thoughtful expression for curiosity, because she promptly trained her attention on me. "Come!" She waved her hand at the door with a flourish. "This street is far too loud and distracting. There are too many auras to get a clear reading. We'll consult the cards to find out the nature of this secret you must find. Madam Dianne will do it free, just for today. I'm also offering a discount on amber necklaces. They drive away negative karma."

"No, thanks." I gave the woman a polite nod and turned to leave. I just wanted to get some lunch and unwind from the morning rush. I didn't feel like listening to a woman in clown paint and a bargain bin gypsy costume fabricate my future with some imaginary lover. I let out a gasp as an icy cold hand clamped down on my wrist.

"You must hear what I have to say." The woman stared at me with wide eyes. There was something in the tone that made the hairs on the back of my neck stand up. "There is great trouble coming your way!"

Thyme carefully removed the woman's hand from my arm. The woman didn't have a chance to speak, as Thyme was already pulling me down the street.

"Gracious, she should have made it a drama club," Thyme said with irritation as we started for a nearby café. "Are you all right?"

"I'm fine," I assured her as I glanced over my shoulder. The woman was still watching us from the doorway like a spook from a bad horror movie. "That was an experience."

"Dead grandparents, difficult mother-daughter relationships, and men who hide something from their partners—talk about pandering to clichés. If she was going to do a cold read, she should have read up on how to do it first."

"A cold read?" I was new to magic and the paranormal.

"It's a trick used by stage artists," Thyme explained. "There are actually psychic people, as you know, but there are also fakes. Fakes use cold reads to make it look like they are reading you. The good ones make a general statement and watch your body language. In fact, it's all about body language and calculated guesses."

I looked at her blankly.

"Okay," Thyme continued. "How are you today?"

"Fine." My response was automatic. It had been a busy morning, and it was hard not to be affected by the weird encounter with the strange woman. I frowned and rubbed my temples.

Thyme laughed. "You say you're fine, but there is great unease around you. You have met with an unusual occurrence today, have you not?"

"I get it now. Cold read?"

"Yep. That's the part where you would've blurted out your day or given clues that you were stressed, like you just did. They get a feel for your personality based on how you talk, what you say, and how you move, and then give you prompts. They're a cross between psychologists and body language interpreters. You never even realise that you're the one filling in the blanks for them."

"So it's fake?" I was a little disappointed at the idea that the amazing reads I had seen on TV might be a game.

Thyme shook her head. "No. Intuition is real. The point is that not everyone who claims to have psychic ability actually does."

"She sounded awfully convincing about trouble coming, though." I was uneasy. As outlandish as the woman was, something about that moment really bothered me.

"Don't worry about it. It was just a bunch of badly crafted drama." Thyme waved a hand dismissively and gave me a wide smile. "And my grandparents don't need to bother spirits to say they love me. They email me every other week."

I grinned at that, but something about the

woman's words kept nagging at me. *There is great trouble coming your way.*

"Seriously, don't worry about it," Thyme said again when she saw my worried expression. "She was wrong about everything else. How accurate could a drama queen in a cheap Cher wig be?"

CHAPTER 2

$\mathcal{W}$hen I arrived back at my house, the crazy woman's words were still whirling around in my mind. What did Madam Dianne mean when she said that something terrible was looming ahead of me?

I walked up the pathway towards my front door. As I passed the large lilac tree in the front yard, I saw what looked like a hand jutting out into view on the porch.

I caught my breath, the woman's words foremost in my mind. I was scared to get a glimpse of what was waiting for me at the front door. With the bushes obstructing most of the porch, I couldn't see enough of the object to make out what I was staring at from a distance. When I was just a few steps away, a prone figure came into view.

I stumbled backwards in horror. A motionless body lay sprawled out in front of the door to my house.

I gingerly approached the body, my heart beating fast. At that moment, my two cats ran up to me and meowed. Hawthorn, my big, black cat, looked up at me and hissed before looking back down at the body. The ginger and white cat, Willow, hissed at the body and then darted off into the bushes.

I forced myself to look at the body. The pale, bluish tone of the body's skin caused my skin to crawl. I reached for the man's wrist and touched it with two fingers. There was no pulse, and the body was so cold that it sent shivers down my spine.

I shook my head and tried to think what to do next. The first thing that crossed my mind was that my house might have killed the man. Perhaps he was robbing the house, and the house spat him out a little too violently. I shuddered at the thought. And what about the cats? They were reacting weirdly. "What did you do now?" I asked the house.

Obviously, I had to call the cops, but I figured I should get help from my neighbour, Camino, first. If the house had something to do with it, I needed to speak to her before the cops looked around.

I took off next door to the elderly woman's home. When the front door opened, Camino stood there, her hair up in curlers as she greeted me with a big smile. "Hello, there. Wait, what's wrong?" She motioned for me to come inside.

I shook my head and swallowed the lump in my throat. "I just got home and found a man lying on my front porch. His skin was pale and cold. He doesn't have a pulse. He's dead! What if the house did it?" I covered my face with my hands and then massaged my temples.

Camino, however, seemed to take the news calmly. "Well, I can assure you that your house had nothing to do with that," she said slowly. "Houses don't kill people. Not even yours."

"Maybe it's not just the house," I said with mounting hysteria. "What if the cats did it?"

Camino shook her head. "Your familiars certainly aren't to blame, either," she said. "They are spiritual creatures that can sense things that you and I just don't understand until it's too late. They were probably watching over the body."

I sighed. "Well, who is that man and why is he on my front porch?"

"That's something that I couldn't possibly answer. Have you ever met this man before?" she asked me. "Perhaps he had business for the store or something?"

"I don't believe so," I replied. "Anyway, what do we do now?"

Camino frowned. "You haven't called the police?"

I shook my head, feeling like an idiot. "No, I wanted to speak to you first. I was worried that the house did it. I mean, what if he was robbing the place and the house overreacted?"

"I'm sure the house didn't do it," she said, "but let's go back and have a look before you call them."

We got back to find the cats were still on the porch, but rather than being calm and quiet like earlier, Hawthorn was happily chasing Willow around, leaping to and fro as if the body wasn't even there.

"At first, all I could see was what looked like a hand sticking out. I guess I'm happy that it wasn't just a hand, though," I added.

"Did you happen to see any marks or anything on the body?" Camino asked, crouching beside the corpse.

"No, I didn't, but this means that Madam Dianne was right," I said.

Camino raised an eyebrow. "Who is Madam Dianne?"

"Oh, she's the woman that opened the psychic store in town. She told me that she saw something terrible ahead of me. This must be what she meant."

Camino sighed and shook her head. "That woman is probably selling a load of nonsense and nothing more. I wouldn't lend any credence to her words."

I bit my lip. "Maybe, since she did get every-thing else wrong, but it's still a strange coincidence, isn't it?"

"Aren't all coincidences strange?" Camino replied.

"I guess so, but it's still a bit spooky."

Camino shrugged. "At any rate, the house didn't do this," she said. "Call the police now."

I pulled my mobile phone from my jeans pocket and made the call. After several rings, a voice greeted me on the other end. "Bayberry Creek police. How may I help you?"

"I just came home to find a dead body on my front porch!"

CHAPTER 3

I looked up at Camino and frowned. "The police will be here soon. What about the house? If we go inside, will it attack them or something if it feels like I'm being threatened?" I asked, with rising panic.

Camino shook her head. "Not a chance. That just isn't how it works, Amelia. Relax, and everything will work out fine."

"But we know the house doesn't like certain people."

Camino interrupted me. "Trust me. Nothing will happen. The house is not going to harm the police, and it sure didn't have anything to do with the man on your porch."

I looked at her and sighed. "I know you're right,

but I'm just so worried. Why was that man at my door?"

Before Camino could answer, two police cars pulled over in front of the house, and officers hurried over to us.

"We received an emergency call from this address," an officer in a sergeant's uniform said. "We have a report of a deceased person on your property, is that correct? And may I ask which of you is the homeowner?" He pulled a small notepad and pen from his pocket.

"I am," I replied. "This is my next door neighbour, Camino."

The sergeant nodded. "Do you know the name of the deceased party?"

Camino and I exchanged glances. "I've never seen him before in my life," I said.

The cop scratched his chin. "Hmm," he murmured. "I'll ask both of you to stay here while we do a preliminary examination of the body, and then we'll need to speak with both of you. We'll need to search your house, if you have no objection."

"Sure." I handed him my keys, and hoped that they wouldn't do anything to offend the house.

The sergeant joined the others on the porch while Camino and I remained on the grass. "You don't think they suspect me, do you?" I whispered.

Camino shook her head. "Of course not. They're just doing their jobs. If you don't calm down a little, they might think otherwise, though. Just let things happen as they are meant to."

The same police officer soon walked back over. "Was your door locked when you first discovered the body, or did you go inside before calling us?" the sergeant asked.

"No. As far as I know, it was already locked from earlier. I made sure the door was secure when I left this morning," I replied. "I haven't been inside since I found him."

"You are certain you haven't seen this man before?"

I nodded. "Yes, I've never seen him before."

The sergeant scribbled in his notepad. "We found a realtor's license in the man's pocket that shows that he's from out of town."

"That just makes it even stranger," I said.

The sergeant frowned. "Can you explain what you mean?"

"I mean, why would some random man travel a

few towns over or whatever, just to show up on the doorstep of someone he had never met?" I asked.

"That's exactly what we have to find out," he replied. "The forensic people are on their way. When they remove the body from the scene, you'll be able to go back to your routine."

"Thanks, but what about until then? Can I go inside my house?"

The cop looked over at the porch for several seconds and then turned back to me. "Hold on just one second. I'll have a word with Constable Walker."

I strained my ears to overhear what the police were saying, but the only words I could make out were, "There's nothing inside as far as evidence goes."

The sergeant's next words were louder. "Constable Walker, you're going to be in charge of questioning the older woman. I'll speak to the homeowner. Tell the others to make sure that nobody steps near that body until forensics arrives."

The sergeant walked back to us and nodded to the front door. "We can head inside now."

When I passed the body, I did my best to avert my eyes.

Constable Walker took Camino into another

room, and the sergeant scribbled on his pad. "Where were you earlier today? You mentioned that you locked up before leaving. Where did you go?"

"Excuse me?" I asked, caught off guard by the question.

"We don't yet have a precise time of death, but the lack of rigor mortis points to a short timeline. The victim was probably dead for a couple hours at most before you reported it, so we need to know your whereabouts during that time."

I froze, my mind going blank. I couldn't help but feel that the sergeant suspected me. My heart beat faster and faster as my anxiety increased. "I was with my friend, Thyme. We went shopping and then had lunch. Why did he die? Was it a heart attack?"

The sergeant tilted his head and squinted. "Would you say that for the last three to four hours, you were with your friend rather than here?"

I noted that he hadn't answered my question. "Yes," I said. "You can check with her."

"I will. And you say that you've never seen him before? So you would have no reason or motive for killing him?"

My jaw fell. "Of course not!" I said, a little too loudly.

"These questions are just routine, miss. That will be all for now."

CHAPTER 4

I was sweeping the floor when the bell above the door chimed, and a customer walked in. It was towards the end of the day. Business had been steady, but was now dying down. I craned my neck, and saw Madam Dianne, the fortune teller. The woman came in quickly, a flurry of scarves and the sleeves of her flowing dress billowing out behind her. She certainly dressed like a fortune teller; I had to give her that.

Thyme was in the back, cleaning the kitchen, so I leant the broom and dustpan against the wall and hurried around behind the counter.

"Hey, Madam Dianne," I said with a smile. "What can I get you?"

Dianne smiled back, but it was a slight and forced smile, her lips barely turning upwards at the corners. "I need cake, or cupcakes. Or both," she said, her voice wavering.

I looked her over. The woman was obviously distraught, but we barely knew one another. I didn't think it would be proper for me to ask if she was all right, so I nodded and reached for a box. "Well, we have plenty of both," I said, trying to sound upbeat.

"What's this one?" Dianne asked, pressing the end of her index finger against the glass front of the case.

I bent and opened a sliding door at my side, so I could peer into the case and see which one she was pointing at. It was a cake, small and round, sitting on the bottom shelf. "Oh, that's our triple chocolate cake."

"Triple chocolate?" Dianne asked.

"Yes. Chocolate cake with a fudge core, and chocolate icing."

"I need chocolate," Dianne said, nodding softly. "I'm having dizzy spells." She suddenly pressed a hand to her nose, as if she were stopping a sneeze, although I figured Dianne was actually trying to keep her tears at bay.

For the most part she succeeded, but one fat drop of salty water leaked from the corner of her right eye and ran down her cheek, leaving a wet line down her face.

I didn't know whether or not to offer consolation, as I was still unsure how she would react if I did. "Did you want a slice, or the whole cake?"

"The whole thing," Dianne said. "And I'll have two of whatever those cupcakes are there, the ones with the purple icing."

I nodded and boxed up the cake, and then got a smaller box for the cupcakes. I boxed them up as well and placed both boxes on the top of the counter. "Is there anything else?" I asked.

Dianne took one look at the boxes and then the tears came. Her sobbing was as loud as her tears were seemingly unending.

I stood rooted to the floor, unsure what I should do, and then went out behind the counter and patted Dianne on the shoulder. It had no effect whatsoever.

The swinging door that led to the back room burst open, and Thyme barrelled into the storefront. "Good gravy, what's going on?" she asked before she got a good look at anything.

"Dianne's here. She's upset," I said, stating the obvious as the woman's wails had risen to high volume.

"What's wrong?" Thyme asked, hurrying over to Dianne.

"It's horrible!" Dianne wailed, speaking when she could between sobs.

Thyme took Dianne by the arm. "Let's get you some tea."

While Thyme took Dianne out the back, I hurried to the front of the store and locked the door, and then swung around the orange and black 'Open' sign to read 'Closed.'

When I made it to the back room, I found Thyme at the stove, heating water in a kettle on a burner. Dianne was sitting on a small folding chair next to the table. She was still crying, although it seemed as though she was getting herself together.

"So what's wrong?" Thyme asked her.

"The police came to my store today," Dianne said. "Thomas Hale was killed."

"Did you know him?" I asked.

"Of course," Dianne said. "We both lived in Newcastle before moving here."

Thyme and I exchanged glances. "You moved here together?" I asked her. Newcastle was a major city, and no one would know everyone in their own suburb, let alone in the entire city.

"What? No, nothing like that," Dianne said,

shaking her head. Her black curls swirled so violently that I thought they would fly off.

Thyme set the tea in front of Dianne and then sat in the chair across from her.

"You both happened to move here and knew each other?"

"I didn't know him—I just knew of him. I heard he was moving here, and I knew he was a realtor, so I asked him to help me find a place, because I had decided to move here as well. He actually sold my house back home, too. My old home, I should say."

I blinked. That was quite a coincidence. "So why did the police speak to you? Why were you so upset?"

"They came to my store, and then they took me to the police station. They said Thomas was murdered! They weren't just asking questions!" Dianne insisted, and then, after she sucked in another breath, she wailed, "I'm a suspect!" She took a sip from the mug of tea, and that seemed to calm her. I figured it was chamomile tea, with perhaps some valerian.

"That doesn't mean you're a suspect," Thyme said in a placating tone.

"Oh, yes it does," Dianne said. "I knew him. I

came to Bayberry Creek. I asked him to go to the house he was killed at."

"What?" I screeched.

"I saw the house on one of my trips here, when I was deciding whether or not to move here. I drove through some years ago and fell in love with the place. I knew this town was perfect for my shop. I can sense things, you know. The years went by, and I never forgot it. When you have my gift, it just comes out. I know that the man you'll marry already has his eye on you," Dianne said, nodding at me.

I frowned.

"And you, Thyme," she continued, "I know that you look up to your boss here, and you desperately hope that one day you will be as good a baker as she is. I know you will be! I can see it."

I had to fight to keep from laughing. Thyme was shaking and had her hand pressed over her mouth, so I knew she was having trouble, too. Yet despite my amusement, I wanted to know about my house. "Why did you send him to the house?"

"I wanted that house. I've got my shop, and there's a tiny apartment above it that I'm staying in now, but I want to buy that home. It's a lovely Victorian one. I asked Thomas to see if it was available, and he said he would go to the owner and ask. He was a kind man, you know. I sensed good things for him ahead. He was going to come into some money. But people can change things, and now he won't come into money, or anything good." She sniffled again.

"So, you can see things, but they might not come true?" Thyme asked sceptically.

"Yes. But if you're worried about the baking thing, I'm telling you, some day you really will be just as talented at baking as Amelia is."

"Thanks. I was worried about that," Thyme said with a barely suppressed chuckle.

Dianne mopped her eyes. "This is horrible. I'm a suspect, but I'm not a murderer!"

Thyme and I murmured words of sympathy, but Dianne cut us off. "You two are going to help me. I can see that in our futures." She took another sip of tea and then set down her half empty cup.

"That's my house, you know," I said.

Dianne looked up at me, puzzled.

"The house you wanted to buy," I said. "The Victorian. That's my house. I live there."

"Amelia is the one who found the body," Thyme said.

I shot Thyme a look, expecting the pronouncement to upset Dianne, but on the contrary, the woman stopped crying altogether. She fixed me with a steely gaze, her eyes glittering. "You found Thomas Hale's body?" she asked me. "And that was your house? He died at your house?" Her face filled with shock, and something else I couldn't quite put my finger on.

She stood up abruptly. "Thank you for every-thing. We can speak tomorrow." She rushed for the front door.

I followed her to unlock the door, and then locked it behind her. It was now past closing time. When I turned, I saw Thyme leaning against the end of the counter.

"She didn't pay for those cakes, did she?"

I shrugged. "She was upset. I couldn't say anything."

Thyme laughed. "I'm surprised she didn't tell you that she saw you losing money."

CHAPTER 5

The first thing the following morning, Thyme was showing me, for the umpteenth time, how to make cupcakes. I really don't know why she bothered. I knew it was going to be a disaster.

The ringing as the front door opened signalled a customer. "Saved by the bell," I said smugly, setting down the flour. The disaster was averted, or at least delayed.

The customer was none other than Dianne. "I feel faint," she announced loudly, taking off her raincoat and shaking droplets of water all over my newly washed floor. "I'd like a dozen chocolate peanut butter cupcakes, please." She jabbed her finger on the display cabinet.

"Are you still having dizzy spells?" I asked her.

She nodded. "It's the police. I'm just so stressed because they obviously see me as a suspect. It's just not fair. By the way, I Friended you on Facebook last night."

I smiled at her. "Yes, I accepted."

"Thanks," she said. "Why don't you have any photos on Facebook? Your profile picture is of two cats."

"I'm camera shy." I accepted the money from her, thankful that she had actually paid this time.

"A pretty girl like you? If I looked like you, I'd have my photos all over my Facebook page. As it is, I don't use Facebook much."

I smiled at her. I wondered if that was why her Facebook privacy settings were so high. Plus there was the fact that she didn't have any posts at all.

"Your grandmother was very fond of cats," she said. "I mean your mother's mother. She loved cats. She always had plenty of them running around the house."

"She was allergic to cats," I said without thinking, and then gave myself a mental kick for being so tactless.

Dianne shook her head. "That was when she was older. Madam Dianne sees all. She had plenty of cats when she was younger. You just didn't know about that."

I shrugged. I knew for a fact that my grandmother had been diagnosed at an early age with a severe allergy to cats, and consequently had an aversion to cats all her life.

Dianne was still speaking. "You inherited your love of cats from your grandmother. Her favourite cat was called Oktoberfest, named after her German ancestry and her love of beer."

"My grandmother?" I asked incredulously. My grandmother had Irish ancestry on both sides, no German ancestors whatsoever, and was a strict teetotaller Baptist.

"Yes," Dianne said forcefully. "Obviously there was a lack of communication between you and your grandmother."

I nodded and did my best not to laugh. I boxed up the cupcakes and handed them to her.

"Madam Dianne senses that you, not Thyme, made these cupcakes," she said. "I sense that they are even better than all your usual cupcakes."

"Thanks," I said, still trying to keep a straight face.

Before she made it to the door, two men hurried into the shop.

I looked up, but the smile froze on my face. They were two stern-looking men, and the shorter one was holding out his badge to Dianne.

"Ms Dianne Longley?"

Dianne nodded and took a step backwards.

"I'm Detective Harrison, and this is Detective Sassafras of the Homicide Squad," the taller one said sternly, closing his big black umbrella with a snap.

I felt guilty, and I hadn't even committed a crime.

"You might be able to help us with the investigation into Thomas Hale's murder," Harrison continued.

"Me?" Dianne squealed. The poor woman was obviously terrified.

"We'd like you to accompany us back to the station to help us with our inquiries," the other detective said.

Dianne ran behind the counter to me. She threw her arms around my neck and gripped tightly. "Help me!" she said dramatically.

I struggled to breathe, and pulled her arms from my throat. "Don't worry," I said. "You're not being arrested or anything. Is she?" I asked the cops.

"No," Detective Harrison said.

That did not seem to placate Dianne at all. She reached for my wrists. "Please help me, Amelia. I'm all alone in the world. Promise that you'll help me! Say the words!"

"I'll help you," I said. I had no idea how, but my heart went out to her. I knew what it was like to be alone. "Don't forget your cupcakes."

"Ms Spelled, we will be speaking to you later," Sassafras said, pointing to me.

I winced, and handed the box to Dianne. She left with the police, casting a terrified look over her shoulder as they escorted her out the door. I headed for the swinging doors to tell Thyme what had happened, but was forestalled by the front door opening once more.

It was Kayleen, the mail lady, and she had never once bought a cake from my store. The day was rapidly heading downhill. "Hi Kayleen," I said warily.

"Are you trying to avoid me?" she snapped.

I was puzzled. "No, why do you say that?"

"Don't answer a question with a question," she barked. "It's a sure sign of guilt. You're never home when I deliver the mail."

"That's because I'm always here at work," I

said, unable to keep the exasperation out of my voice.

Kayleen appeared to be digesting that for a moment. "Oh, I see," she said after an interval. "I just thought you had a good hiding place. I couldn't see you when I looked through your windows."

"You looked through my windows?"

Kayleen shrugged. "Yes, but I think you should stop spraying for cockroaches, or whatever it is that you do. I always get sick near your house. I think I'm allergic."

I nodded. "Well, I must get back to work."

Kayleen ignored me. "Did you hear what killed that man you found?"

Now she had my interest. "No, what killed him?"

"Insulin!" Kayleen proclaimed triumphantly. "A big shot of insulin!"

I narrowed my eyes. "Are you sure?"

Kayleen winked at me. "I own the courier service here too, you know, not just the mail contract. Anyway, my girlfriends and I are going to Coffs Harbour next Monday. Wanna come?"

"I'd love to," I lied. "Thanks for asking, but I can't shut the shop."

Kayleen was visibly affronted. "It will do you

good," she said angrily. "You need to take some time off."

"I can't afford to shut the shop." I said it firmly but politely.

"I knew it!" Kayleen yelled. "You *are* trying to avoid me! I'll get you for this!" She stormed out of the shop, almost knocking down a customer on her way.

I served the customer, and was just heading out to the kitchen to fill in Thyme on the news, when the phone rang. "Help me!" Dianne's voice screeched on the other end. "The police have just searched my house! They think I did it!"

I did the only thing I could do. I ate a double chocolate cupcake with cream cheese icing in one shot.

CHAPTER 6

"*T*hyme, the caramel icing is amazing." I closed my eyes as I savoured a second bite of the sample cupcake.

"The salt really makes a difference." Thyme frosted a set of cupcakes with swirling spirals of the pale brown icing. "Salted caramel's a pretty popular summer treat here. It ought to help draw in more traffic."

I nodded as I swallowed the last of my cupcake. Of course, if this kept up I would have to start my morning runs again. These sweets were going to expand my waistline before I knew it. Thyme's cupcakes were just too tasty to resist trying. How in the world did she get it right the first time?

"Do you want to try to make a batch?" Thyme waved a hand towards the leftover ingredients scattered over the counter. "Your sponge cake there wasn't anywhere near as bad as usual."

"I know you're joking," I said. I nervously studied the cake cooling on the wire rack. It looked normal enough, if a bit on the flat side. Well, if you can call a big hole in the middle 'flat.' Plus there was the fact that it had squashed the metal cooling rack. It looked like a giant donut gone wrong, complete with thick charred edges.

Thyme waved a spatula at me. "All righty, but you're not getting out of making the glaze. Even if you can't cook, icing will be a big help this weekend."

I nodded. At least I was able to make the glaze. It was hard to mess up butter cream, so I was glad I would be able to contribute somewhere. Still, the marzipan and fondant were going to take some getting used to. Until I had taken over ownership of the cake store, I had never realised how many types of icing there were.

"The cakes should be cool enough to ice by now." Thyme picked up one and broke off a piece. She popped the treat into her mouth and chewed thoughtfully. "Never mind, you might be able to make some passable cakes soon."

"Don't start looking for a new job, yet," I warned her.

"Oh, don't worry. I'm not going anywhere anytime soon," Thyme said as the bell alerted us to a new customer.

My pulse quickened, and I quickly chided myself for my reaction. But truth be told, the view was fantastic. Craig looked as rugged and handsome as ever with his work jacket tossed casually over one shoulder. I found myself wondering how he could possibly be single. Something had to be wrong. My thoughts ran away with me—multiple personalities? An extra toe or two? A house overrun with display cases of Barbie dolls? Live taipans or other deadly snakes as pets?

"Hey." Craig gave a quirked grin.

"Hi." A wave of mortification hit me when the high squeak leaked into my voice. Serves me right for ogling. What was wrong with me? I cleared my throat and gave him a bright smile. "Sorry, I'm a little hoarse today. How are you?"

"Good." To my relief, Craig seemed more amused than anything. He bent over to study the cupcakes.

The phone rang and I half turned to see Thyme hurrying to answer it. "Fingers crossed, I might have my own cakes out soon. I just need to make them edible first."

Craig gave a good-natured laugh. "Well, let me know if you do. I'd like to boast about being first in line when you sold your first cakes here."

"You got it." My shoulders relaxed as I settled into the more familiar chit chat. "What can I do for you today?"

Craig shot me a winning smile. "We have a new officer in the department. I've volunteered to pick up cakes to celebrate her surviving orientation. You know how we are. Any excuse to unwind a little."

"Nothing wrong with that." I grinned and looked over the display. "There's some biscotti, too. Maybe a couple of those to go with someone's coffee would be an idea?"

"That sounds good. Give me a dozen of those, and a half dozen of the chocolate cupcakes."

"You got it." I reached for the boxes to pack the treats for his order. "Anything else?"

"That should do it for today."

Before he could say anything else, a man hurried in. "What's the soup of the day?"

I shook my head. "We're a cake store."

The man seemed puzzled. "You're not a diner?"

"No," I said politely. "We're a cake store."

"So you don't sell coffee, or soup?"

"No," I said, "just cakes. We're a cake store."

The man's brows furrowed, and he left, muttering to himself.

Craig looked over his shoulder at the cake shaped logo painted on the glass door. He looked back at me and pointed at the logo.

I just gave a sigh and a half shrug. "Apparently the sign is a tad vague for some. It happens all the time."

He shook his head, and then frowned. "Is everything all right, after, well, you know, the body at your house?"

I nodded. I tried not to let the image of the crumpled body on my porch resurface as I took his payment. "Everything's fine. I still don't know what happened to him, though."

"Well, you let me know if you need anything."

My chest tightened as Craig stared into my eyes. "It'll all work out. One day at a time."

"No truer words," Craig agreed as he picked up the boxes and balanced them on one broad forearm. "You take care of yourself. No more fires while you experiment back there."

"No promises." I smiled as I reluctantly watched him go. It was always so easy to chat with him when he made the fire department's cake run.

Thyme gave her shoulder a friendly slap. "Way to ruin a perfect opportunity."

"Say what?" I looked at her in confusion.

"Everything's fine," Thyme imitated me in an overly perky tone. She sighed dramatically. "Would tossing the guy a bone kill you? If you'd said you needed someone to talk to, he'd have asked if you were free for coffee or something. He was totally scoping an excuse."

"Don't be silly, Thyme." I cleaned the crumbs from the counter.

"I'm not being silly. I know he likes you. You guys are so transparent that it's painful to watch." Thyme snagged the washcloth in mid air and nudged me out of the way with a hip bump. "And after I sacrificed my cupcakes for you to chat him up! I gotta start a new tray now. Anyway, you're improving. You made a cake and didn't even set off the fire alarm. Go with it." She grinned. "You'll be a baker before you know it."

"Not by this weekend, though. How am I supposed to help with fifteen cakes when I can't tell salt from sugar?"

Thyme winced slightly and forced a smile. "Fourteen. That call was a cancelation."

"Really?" I frowned, torn between the disappointment of lost business and relief it was one less burden on Thyme this weekend. "Did they say what happened?"

"Word spreads fast. They heard about the body on your porch and…" Thyme's voice trailed away with a sigh. "Some people are ridiculous. Don't let them get to you."

Before I could press for details, the door chimed. I turned to see the two detectives who had come for Madam Dianne.

"Detectives Harrison and Sassafras," the taller one said, nodding to me. "Ms Amelia Spelled." He was staring at me as if I were an insect under a microscope. "Could we sit and talk?"

I felt a pang of dread. No good news ever came from sitting to talk with the cops.

As soon as we reached the back room, Detective Harrison wasted no time coming to the point. "The victim's name was Thomas Hale. Does the name ring a bell at all?"

"No. I've never heard of anybody by that name. Well, I've heard of him now, of course, because it's all over town. I had never heard of him when I found him, though; that's what I mean."

"He was a new resident. He arrived in town last week to work as a realtor for Bayberry Creek Realty. Do you recall ever having the company approach you about the house while you were settling in? Did you maybe see a letterhead or a business card in your aunt's belongings?"

I shook my head. "Sorry, no. Dianne Longley did tell me that she'd hired him to approach me about the possibility of selling my house. He died before he could get in touch with me, obviously."

The second cop studied me with concern. "Mr Hale had a notebook of your work hours as well as photos of you and your house in his motel room."

"He had my what?" I felt my voice tighten into a sharp squeak as a wave of anxiety overcame me. I could understand him having photos of my house, but of me? Some strange man had a photo of me in his motel room. I hated having my photo taken. I would twist, run, crouch, and crab walk sideways to avoid a camera. I had chased down friends to delete ill-gotten selfies from their phones. What was this man doing with photos of me?

"They were likely provided to him by the company. Maybe from your social media pages."

"No," I said sharply. "I have no photos of myself online. None." A cold chill passed down my spine at the thought. Had people taken photos of me without me knowing? What in the world was going on? "A strange man has photos of me—what does this mean?"

"Likely nothing, Ms Spelled. He was probably assigned to approach you about selling your house, or he might have been acting independently, given that Ms Longley had engaged him to approach you."

"But he had my photos." I was concerned.

"I wouldn't worry too much about it, Ms Spelled. He can't use them where he's at." He paused and removed his glasses to wipe them clean. "You could always file a complaint with his office, if you feel the photos were in violation of your privacy."

"No. No, that's all right." As creepy and weird as it was to have perfect strangers keeping notes about me and my house, a dispute would go nowhere given that the man was deceased.

The man also had a note of my hours. If I hadn't gone shopping with Thyme, I likely would have been there when the man collapsed. Madam Dianne's face came to mind as the cops droned on about the various formalities, asking me to sign a statement to affirm my claims.

"There is great trouble coming your way." Her voice echoed in the back of my mind as I tried to focus on the forms in front of me.

Why did the dead man have photos of me?

CHAPTER 7

*R*uprecht Foxtin-Flynn's shop, *Glinda's*, had a way of making a person feel welcome, even on a dreary, overcast day. The air was heavy with rain that refused to fall. The trees seemed to droop in depression from the sun's absence. Not even the birds were out in this weather.

Yet *Glinda's* was completely unaffected by its gloomy surroundings. In fact, it was the most cheerful looking building on the street. The 'Open' sign beckoned in an inviting handwritten script.

The red brick stones and the heavy burgundy curtains in the window made the rest of the street look drab and lifeless by comparison. I could not help but wonder if the shop had some sort of life of its own, like my house. Well, a more social one of course. It wouldn't do to have a shop that booted people out at every turn. I smiled to myself as I imagined shoplifters suddenly finding themselves out on the footpath.

I was jolted from my thoughts when the door opened with a cheerful jingle of silver bells tied to the handle.

"Amelia, what are you doing standing out there in the damp? You'll catch pneumonia!" Mint, Ruprecht's granddaughter, gave me a welcoming smile as she scolded me, waving for me to come inside. "Come on in!"

"Sorry, I was lost in thought." I balanced the plastic tray between my hands.

"I wouldn't know why you would have so much to think about. Things have been so dull and tranquil since you moved to town." Mint winked at me before looking up at the sky and waving me in insistently. "Come inside before it starts to pour."

As if to emphasise her point, thunder rumbled in the distance. I hurried inside and handed her the tray. "I hope sandwiches are okay. I wasn't quite bold enough to cook anything."

"These were so thoughtful! Thank you,

Amelia." Mint accepted the tray and closed the door. "I have some tea brewing. How about you join the others at the table?"

Before long everyone was chattering around the table. No matter how many times I came by, I always felt that the place was truly magical. The shelves lining the walls were all wood, but not the glue-and-sawdust-from-the-store type. They were true blue heavily polished wood. Each one was hand carved with intricate Celtic knots and swirling vines, and each leaf was chiselled out in exquisite detail.

The table must have been made by the same craftsman. The dark cherry wood gleamed in the light that came from a myriad of candles, giving this particular room a special ambiance.

The books on the shelves were all leather bound. Most of them looked ancient. Mint had explained that this room was for private gatherings, and housed their rare collectibles for special patrons. There were even display cases with hand-made books dated to the eighteenth century. These were no doubt Ruprecht's pride and joy.

Despite the rows of books, the place did not smell dusty or old at all. The jars of herbs that lined the upper shelves along with the rows of candles gave the place a witchy atmosphere. There was a tapestry on the far wall, depicting a woman and a dragon under a crescent moon. The many candles burning threw the dark blue walls into relief.

Ruprecht smiled as he followed my eyes to the tapestry. "An old friend in England just sent that to me. His daughter crafts them for festivals every year."

"That's amazing!" I gazed enviously at the tapestry. I wished I had half that sort of talent. In fact, I would be happy if I could just ice a cake evenly, and maybe make icing flowers look like more than blobs of abstract colours. "She has amazing talent."

"I'll forward your praise when I talk to them next," Ruprecht said with a smile on his face.

"Has there been any word from Madam Dianne?" Thyme asked as she took a sip of her tea.

I shook my head. "I was thinking of taking her something to eat." I raised my hands in surrender as every head turned in my direction. "Nothing I cooked, of course! I was hoping one of you would suggest something she'd like."

Camino offered me a tray of crackers. "The

diner always has a nice soup. It would be easy on her stomach, given that she must be stressed."

"You could take some cakes from the store," Thyme said. "The plum cake I made yesterday would probably be a treat. Sweet things help make everything better." She gazed up at the ceiling thoughtfully. "Except blood sugar levels, I guess. But other than that, it's a win-win."

"I could cook something, too," Mint chimed in. "We should all go and offer a little distraction from her troubles. She could certainly use it. We could welcome her to town."

"It seems silly that the police would suspect the poor woman. She wouldn't hurt a soul." Camino shook her head in exasperation. "You just can't trust the experts sometimes. They go around looking for a quick answer, not necessarily the right one."

Ruprecht studied the inside of his cup. He was unusually quiet as we chattered on. I wondered what was going on in his mind.

"Well, is there anything we can do?" I looked around the table for inspiration.

"We could make a small casserole and make sure she knows she is in our thoughts." Mint tapped her finger on the hardwood table in contemplation.

"No. I mean, anything we can *do*. With, you

know." I felt weird, trying to request a spellcasting on Dianne's behalf. However, if they could use magic to spy on suspects and make magic love-cupcakes, well, surely they could be of some use in the situation.

"It's not that simple," Camino said cautiously. "We could do a truth spell, I suppose, to make the truth come to light. And a protection spell over Dianne, too."

"If we had some sort of evidence to work with, maybe we could achieve a better result," Thyme mused.

"So if there was some sort of evidence to work with, we might be able to clear her name?" I prompted the group.

Ruprecht stroked his chin. "There's nothing to say that we couldn't."

"Nothing guarantees it, either," Camino added.

"We could still do a spell of clarity." Thyme waved a cracker to emphasise her point, but Mint shook her head.

"But clarity for what?" Mint wagged a finger in denial. "There are plenty of things we could accidentally bring clarity to that are better left unknown. We could easily cause more harm than good."

"True." Thyme chewed her bottom lip as she mulled over the problem. "Clarity as to who killed him? That seems pretty much to the point."

"Agreed," Ruprecht said as he tilted his cup from side to side, studying its bottom with interest, and then set it down. "But we will lend aid when our part becomes clear. For now, let us simply enjoy each other's company."

"But how will we know?" I asked. I desperately wanted to help Dianne. After all, I knew what it was like to have the community turn on me over a false assumption. But what could I possibly do? I knew even less about magic than I did about baking. I didn't even know spells were real until shortly after I'd moved to Bayberry Creek.

"It will come to you, my dear." Camino gave my hand a reassuring pat. "Sometimes just believing in someone is all the magic you need to help them through hard times. There isn't a spell in existence that makes better medicine."

"Though spells can be very useful when they work the way you want them to." Thyme grinned at me. "You're from a powerful bloodline. Maybe you're accidentally hexing your cooking?"

"Very funny!" I pretended to toss a grape at her.

"Well, think about it!" Thyme laughed. "Your

one and only success was a super deluxe, love potion infused cake. Maybe you're unconsciously trying to spell your cakes to be tasty and it gets lost in magic-translation somewhere."

"I'd settle for edible!" I said, and my remark was met by scattered laughter from the others. I noticed that they did seem oddly thoughtful over the idea. Surely they weren't seriously putting stock into that tease? I barely knew what magic was, so I could hardly see myself subconsciously putting hocus pocus type stuff onto my cooking. If I did, surely my cakes would be less like toxic waste.

"Edible to whom?" Thyme pressed. "Maybe your cooking is a delicacy on another planet. You might be the next iron chef on Mars."

"I think we'd have to look outside the solar system," I said with a dismissive wave of my hand. I was a terrible cook, but I was certain that I wasn't hexing food.

Thankfully, attention was soon diverted from the sorry subject of my cooking and turned to chatter about recent events. Mint and Thyme were bickering lightly with each other, and Ruprecht appeared to be completely focused on his tea as he stayed out of it. Camino was busying herself with tidying up the snacks as she interjected from time to time like a mother hen, clucking at their behaviour. The scene felt warm, comforting, and secure. I had never felt so comfortable at my own family gatherings.

Ruprecht was right. Magic couldn't beat good company, not by a mile.

CHAPTER 8

"*D*arn it," I said sleepily to no one in particular. There was no one in my room, not even the cats, although of course, the house itself was alive in a way. I rolled over onto my stomach and felt along the floor for the phone.

"Hello, Thyme?" I said groggily. "It's early."

"I know," Thyme said. "I'm sorry."

I could tell at once, even in my half-awake and caffeine deficient state, that Thyme was not herself. Her voice was nasal. It dawned on me what Thyme was calling to say before the words even left her mouth.

"No!" I said, loudly. "No, no, no!"

"I know," Thyme said. "I'm sick. I'm sorry." She sounded congested and tired.

"I could just close for the day," I said. "If I cook, we won't have any cash, ever."

Thyme laughed weakly. "What about hiring someone for the day?"

"Who?"

Thyme didn't have an answer for that.

I wondered why a witch was sick at all. Wasn't there a spell she could do? I had no idea. I really did to need to read up a lot more on the subject. I also needed to look for extra staff members I could call on in such a situation.

I didn't speak to Thyme again until later that morning when she called to ask how I was doing. I had stupidly decided to try to bake, and at the very moment Thyme called, smoke was billowing out of the oven, slipping through the small openings at the edges of the door.

"Hi Amelia, how's it all going?" Thyme asked.

"I have to call you back!" I screeched, hanging up and throwing the phone on the countertop in one fluid motion. I ran to the sink at the back of the room, and pulled a small red extinguisher from the cupboard. I ran back to the oven. When I pulled the door open, the flames leaped at me. Within seconds, the towels on the counter next to the oven were burning.

I pulled the silver pin on the extinguisher and aimed it at the fire, but by the time the extinguisher was empty, the fire was still going, albeit far more weakly. I ran back to the phone and called triple zero.

After the call, I went back to the sink. I filled a large mixing bowl with water, and threw it on the flames. That did the trick, but as I stood in the somewhat blackened kitchen, I heard the faint roar of a siren.

Within minutes, Craig and the other fire fighters were in the kitchen. "I put it out just before you got here," I said lamely.

"Well, we rushed here for nothing then," one of the men said to me. "Always the best kind of call—it means everyone is safe."

Craig came over to me. He looked as hot as usual, his muscles seemingly bulging through his uniform. "There isn't any damage here," he said. "Just make sure that oven's working properly before you use it again. You'd better get it checked out. Otherwise, there's nothing that a good clean up wouldn't fix."

I smiled my gratitude. "No more baking for me, seriously."

When Craig and the other fire fighters left, I

spent the morning scrubbing the kitchen. After all, I was experienced with removing smoke and ash from surfaces.

I shut the shop at lunchtime and headed to a local café to buy soup for Thyme.

The woman who answered the door only vaguely resembled Thyme. Her face was pale, her eyes red, and her hair limp and stringy.

"You look terrible," I said.

"Thanks for the compliment," Thyme said dryly.

"I brought you soup." I carefully held up a paper bag.

"Come in, but don't get too close." Thyme threw herself down on her couch. "So what are you doing here? You didn't burn down the bakery, did you?"

I pulled a face. "Well…"

Thyme's mouth dropped open. "I was kidding! Did you? Another fire?"

"Another fire," I said. "Sorry."

"Sorry? It's your shop. If you want to burn it down so badly, go ahead."

I shrugged. "I don't know what happened. I thought I'd try to bake, but then there were flames. Craig came just after I put it out. I spent ages scrubbing the soot."

"Oh, your boyfriend showed up? Now it all makes sense," Thyme teased me.

"He's not my boyfriend," I said defensively, "and what makes sense?"

"Why you keep setting all of these fires. You want to see the fire fighter Ken doll."

I laughed. "I'm not setting fires on purpose, and don't be mean. He has way more muscles than a Ken doll."

"That's a fair point," Thyme said. "Anyway, I still can't believe you set the place on fire again."

I put my head in my hands. "I'm so embarrassed. I'm an optimist—I think that one day I'll be fine with baking, but perhaps I'll never be able to bake. Anyway, I don't know about Craig. I like him, but I don't really feel a spark there. Do you know what I mean? He's awfully good looking, but there's no chemistry. Still, the Millionaire Matchmaker says chemistry needs time to grow. What do you think?"

I looked back up and saw that Thyme had fallen asleep. Her mouth was open and she was snoring softly. I let myself out and drove back to the cake store, all the while thinking about Craig. He hadn't even asked me out, but what would I do if he did?

When I got back, I left the 'Back in 1 hour' sign

hanging on the doorway. There hadn't been many customers that morning, and I figured I was safe to take a few more minutes to clean up before I opened for the afternoon. I threw away the burned towels, and then tried to clean the charcoal from the cake pan. It proved awfully persistent, so I scrubbed at it with salt.

I jumped when I heard the bell above the door to the front of the store. I was sure I had locked the door.

I stepped through the swinging doors, and to my shock, Alder Vervain was standing in the store.

"We're actually closed. I thought that door was locked," I said. I hadn't meant to sound so abrupt, but the man made me nervous. He was dark and brooding, albeit in an attractive sort of way. And how did he get in? There was something mysterious about him, and I'd had an over supply of mysterious since I'd moved to Bayberry Creek.

"Hello to you, too." He looked amused, which annoyed me for some reason.

"Excuse me?"

"Thomas Hale died in your house, did he not?" His gaze was unwavering.

I shifted nervously from foot to foot. "Well, no," I said defensively. "He was on my porch, not in my house. Anyway, why do you ask? Was he a friend of yours, or something?"

"I'm a private detective."

I gasped at the disclosure. Sure, and I'd never make a poker player, but I had not the faintest clue that he was a private detective.

"Do you find it strange that one man died in your shop, and then another man died at your house?"

"What are you saying?" I didn't like where he was going with this. "They found Brant McCallum's murderer."

"You have to admit it's a strange coincidence," Alder said. "Why you?"

"I don't have a clue. Look, I'm sorry, but we're closed. I'm going to have to ask you to leave."

Alder nodded. "All right. I'll come back tomorrow."

I crossed my arms. "If you'd like to buy something, then by all means come back tomorrow."

Alder smiled, a thin smile that I imagined a storybook wizard would smile, as if he knew something I didn't, something important.

Alder left swiftly. There was a strange stillness to the air after he'd gone, and it made me uneasy.

CHAPTER 9

*W*hen I arrived at work the following morning, Alder Vervain was already there. Part of me was pleased to see him, and that in itself annoyed me.

"You're tenacious," I said. I held the door open for him with my foot after I stepped inside.

Alder walked through the door, tucking a newspaper under his arm. "You don't happen to make donuts in this place, do you?"

"No, just cakes and cupcakes." As usual, he was dressed all in black. The scent of cinnamon, and something I couldn't quite identify, seemed to follow him.

"I don't think I should eat a cupcake for breakfast," he said.

I shrugged. "Donuts aren't really much better."

I walked behind the counter. Of course, he was just a private eye, so he had no jurisdiction anywhere, but there was no harm in answering questions. "Okay, enough of the small talk. What do you want to ask me?"

"Many things." Alder bent to look in the empty display counter. "Do you make the cakes fresh each day?"

I folded my arms. "Is that what you really wanted to ask me?"

Alder shot me a look of appraisal, or so I assumed. "What happened with Brant McCallum?"

I shifted from one foot to another. "As you well know, his fiancée was arrested for his murder. She confessed. I had nothing to do with that."

Alder walked over to the counter. "I heard that you and your friends were investigating. You fancied yourself as detectives."

"Where did you hear that?"

"I have my sources," he said.

"Look, my friends and I did investigate, but that was only because the death in my shop was affecting the business. I certainly wouldn't say that we fancied ourselves as detectives or anything like that."

"I see." Alder leant on the counter.

Silence hung in the air between us, making me more and more tense. I was the one to break the silence. "I don't understand why you're asking me questions when you know I had nothing to do with it."

Alder straightened up. "I'm just trying to get a feel for this whole situation. A man is dead—his body shows up on your doorstep. Previously a man dropped dead in your bakery. You have to admit that it sounds rather weird."

"I suppose it does."

"And we both know you don't do the baking here. When exactly does your employee come in?"

Again, I tried not to show surprise on my face. Again, I failed.

"Sources," Alder said simply. He still seemed to be amused. "My client thinks you have something to do with all the things going on here lately. You show up in town; a man dies in your shop; you get your friends together and you all play Scooby Doo or something like that, but it works out okay. Now another man has died, this time at your house, and you're going to get the crew back together and solve another mystery. Is that it? My client wonders if there's more to it than that. I shouldn't tell you all that, but to be honest, I like you." He grimaced when he said that, as if liking me was distasteful to him.

I frowned.

"You seem like a nice, normal person," he continued, "and so do your friends. Well, nice if not normal, in their case." He chuckled to himself. "It really does seem as if you're getting caught up in a bad case of wrong time, wrong place. Yet in my experience, that's not real. If someone's in the wrong place, it's because they put themselves there."

"I assure you, it's nothing but wrong time, wrong place with me. I didn't want a man to die in my cake shop or outside my house. Anyway, who is your client?"

"I can't tell you that."

"So someone can pay you to follow me around, to figure out everything about me, to snoop into my private life, and you won't even tell me who it is?"

Alder nodded. "Yes."

I rolled my eyes. "That's not fair."

"Life isn't fair," Alder said smugly.

"Spare me the philosophical musings," I said. "It annoys people. Remember that Socrates was put to death for annoying people."

Alder sighed.

I went on. "Well, do you believe I had nothing to do with Thomas Hale's death?"

Alder tapped his finger on the counter for a while before looking up at me. "I can tell a lot about someone just by watching them. I can tell when they're lying or nervous, for example."

"Oh yes?" I said, interested in spite of myself. "I used to watch that show on TV. I can't remember what it's called. Anyway, there was a man who helped the police, and he could tell if someone was lying. He looked for facial ticks, sweating, stuff like that. Apparently when people lie, they look to the left, but they look to the right if they're trying to remember something. Or is it the other way around?"

"It depends whether they're right or left hand-ed," Alder said, "but that theory's been discounted by scientists."

"But you can tell if someone's lying?"

Alder smiled at me, and when he spoke, for once his voice dripped with charm. "It's a sixth sense I have."

I stared at him to see if he was joking, but his expression did not change. If only I could have such a sixth sense. "Oh," was I could say.

"I know you had nothing to do with the realtor's death," he continued, "and that's what I'm going to tell my client. I'm not so sure they'll agree, so I'm also not so sure you won't be seeing more of me."

I nodded. I was secretly pleased to be seeing more of him, because I felt a magnetic attraction to him, albeit regrettably. He was the cliché tall, dark and handsome, to be sure, but there was something more. He had an almost otherworldly presence. I looked up to see him watching me, and I fervently hoped that mind reading wasn't another of his arcane talents.

"But, like I said, I think it's a waste of time. To tell you the truth, I've made a lot of money wasting my time on things that never pan out, and if this is another case of that, then so be it."

I nodded, because I had no idea how to respond to that. It sounded as if Alder was letting me know he wasn't going to be a problem for me, but that he would be around, watching. I figured I could live with that.

Alder opened his mouth to speak, but he was forestalled by Thyme's entrance. "Thyme," he said stiffly.

She nodded to him. "Alder." Her voice was filled with tension.

Alder left the shop in a hurry, leaving Thyme wringing her hands.

"Are you feeling any better today?" I asked her, wondering if now was the right time to question her about the mysterious Alder Vervain.

"Back to normal, pretty much," she said, but she didn't look normal. She looked shaken. "What did he want?"

I answered her question with a question. "Did you know that he's a private detective?"

Thyme nodded, and walked into the kitchen. "Of course. Small town—everyone knows everyone else's business. Is he investigating you? Or what? He wasn't buying cupcakes."

"Yes, he *is* investigating me!" I exclaimed. "Someone's paid him to, because they think I had something to do with the murder of Thomas Hale."

Thyme turned after setting some mixing bowls on the counter. "He didn't tell you who his employer was by any chance, did he?"

I pulled a face. "No. He asked me some questions."

Thyme put down the flour and looked at me. "Does he think you had something to do with it?" She seemed concerned, but I had no idea why.

"He said he believes me."

Thyme seemed to be thinking that over.

I pressed on. "He said he knows when someone is lying to him. He has a sixth sense about it."

Thyme snorted rudely.

"He knew that I couldn't bake."

"The whole town knows you can't bake!" Thyme exclaimed.

I chuckled. "Too true. I suppose it does look fishy that a man died in my store and then another man died at my house, but I don't know why anyone would be so convinced that I had something to do with it. Anyway, why do you have a problem with Alder Vervain?"

Thyme shot me a look. "Who says I have a problem with…"

I cut her off, holding up my hand. "Come on. I overheard you guys talking about him once, and you acted weird around him."

Thyme chewed her lip. "Well, I suppose you'll have to know sooner or later."

I was growing impatient. "Know what?"

Thyme rubbed her temples and sighed loudly. "Do you know anything about witchcraft laws in Australia?"

"No, how would I? I didn't know anything about witches until I moved to Bayberry Creek."

Thyme waved one hand at me. "Oh, yes, sorry. Well, no one was ever put to death in Australia, or anything like that. No one has ever been success-fully prosecuted for witchcraft in Australia, but a woman was charged with fortune telling in South Australia about sixty years ago. And a law against practicing witchcraft was repealed in the state of Victoria only as recently as 2005, as ridiculous as that sounds. Alder Vervain's family…" She hesitated.

I was frustrated. How bad could it be? "Just spit it out, Thyme."

She nodded. "His family is from a long line of witch hunters."

"What?" I shrieked. "Witch hunters, like in the movies?" Images of Alder with a crossbow and vials of holy water flashed through my mind. He certainly looked the part.

"No. That was too strong a term, I suppose. Alder's family has always opposed the repeal of witchcraft laws in Australia."

I scratched my head. "I still can't see the prob-lem. What am I missing?"

"Alder's family are firmly on a witch hunt, metaphorically and figuratively speaking," Thyme said angrily. "Obviously, they can't have anyone charged with witchcraft in this day and age, so they look for anything they can. They used to complain to the local council authorities about Ruprecht's shop." She stopped and took a deep breath. "I've been speaking in the present tense, but Alder's parents died some time back. They did all sorts of horrible things to Camino, Ruprecht, and my parents, too, years ago. It's left to Alder now."

"What's left to him? What are you saying? What horrible things did they do?"

Thyme folded her arms across her chest. "You name it, they did it. They spread rumours, constantly complained to authorities. They even called the cops with anonymous tips that Ruprecht and Camino were drug dealers. The tax office audited Ruprecht, Camino, and my parents time and time again. Alder's parents really persecuted them."

"But surely none of this happened recently?" I asked her.

Thyme shook her head. "No, but Alder's only just come back to town. He's been watching you, so it seems that he's going to start up again on all of us, taking up where his parents left off. And this time, you're in his sights, too."

CHAPTER 10

*T*hyme and I were in my car. We had closed for the day, and Thyme wanted to turn the tables on Alder by following him. "The best defence is offence," she had said.

I still found it hard to believe that Alder had malicious intent towards me, but then, I was naïve when it came to seeing through people. "He said he believed me," I said once again. "He said he had a sixth sense and could tell when someone was lying. He did seem to believe me. He said he was going to suggest to his employer that they leave me alone."

Thyme slammed on an imaginary brake with her foot when a car pulled out in front of me. Talk about a back seat driver! I wasn't going to comment though, given her current mood. "Amelia, we've already been through this. I don't think there is an employer, and I like told you over and over again, I don't trust him."

I was in two minds about the whole situation. "Well, he did say that he doubted his employer would listen to him."

"See what I mean! That's just a cover, as there is no employer. I bet he made that up!" Thyme shot me a look. "Amelia, I'm really worried about this. He's a private detective now—just be thankful he isn't a cop—and he's snooping. He has his sights set on you. He's going to cause trouble for you. Please tell me that you'll burn protection incense when you're home."

I nodded. "Yes, I'm already in the habit of that now. I always burn Fiery Wall of Protection incense: Dragon's Blood, frankincense and myrrh."

"Good. And you filled those witch bottles like I told you and…"

I interrupted her. "Yes, and I buried them in the front yard."

"Also good. Did you make that protection poppet, the juju doll-baby?"

I slunk down in my seat. "Err, no, sorry. My sewing is almost as bad as my baking."

Thyme snorted with disgust. "It doesn't have to be a work of art! Just sew some fabric into the vague shape of a person, and stuff it with protection herbs from your garden. You have plenty to choose from. You have those big tubs of rue, and then you have plenty of chamomile, lemongrass, and agrimony growing. You could use rosemary or hawthorn for its hair. And there's wormwood!" She tapped my rear view mirror. "You need to hang some of that here. We've already been through this. Protection is the most important thing for witches. Protection first, before everything."

"Sorry." I was truly remorseful. I'd been slack and really would need to up the protection. "Anyway, why are we following Alder if you think he's not being paid to follow me?"

Thyme sighed. I could tell I was really trying her patience. This whole thing with Alder sure was making her uptight. "While I do think it's highly unlikely that someone actually paid him to investigate you, if such a person does exist, then we need to find out who it is."

I pointed to the small container Thyme had been holding. "Hence your whoosie-whatsit."

"Great technical term," she said dryly. "It's actually scrying water, which you would know if you'd been paying attention. It's rainwater collected under the last full moon, and when it's in this black bowl, I can see images. That is, if I have the chance to concentrate," she added pointedly.

"Understood. I'll be quiet now."

"I can't believe that's working," was the next thing I said, ten or so minutes later.

Thyme laughed. "After all you've seen since you arrived at Bayberry Creek, you're really surprised? Turn right at the stop sign."

I shook my head. "I guess not."

"Okay, I think it's that motel there."

I parked out on the road, under a spreading lemon magnolia tree. "Look at those pretty yellow flowers," I said.

"Focus, Amelia, focus. He's here somewhere," Thyme said. "I think it's one of the last rooms."

I was nervous. "I don't want him to see us, and if he really has a sixth sense, or is psychic or whatever, he'll know we're here."

"Well, I don't want to be caught snooping around, either," Thyme said. "The last person I need to make mad is some crazy witch hunter. Still, we have to find out if there's any truth to his claim that someone hired him, and this is probably the only way we'll find out."

Thyme sat in silence for a moment, staring at her scrying water, while I fidgeted in my seat.

Finally, she spoke. "Yes, he's in the very end room, and I'm pretty sure there's a man in there, too."

"Can you tell if he's the one who hired him to follow me?" I asked.

Thyme shook her head. "I have no idea. I assume he'd have several clients. Anyway, I'll find out who the man is."

"You can do that?" I asked, impressed.

She chuckled. "Not with my scrying water. I'll ask Gloria, you know, the waitress at the north café."

"How would she know?"

"Well, her uncle runs the motel, and Gloria's cousin, Stephanie, is the receptionist there."

I nodded. I should have known. Most people in small country towns were related to each other. At least there was always a network that could be counted on to supply plenty of information, whether real or imagined, about people's personal lives.

"There," Thyme said loudly, startling me. "He's on the move."

"On the move? When did you join the army?" I teased her as I turned the key in the ignition and slid down in my seat.

Sure enough, Alder Vervain was heading across

the motel parking lot to his car. He was carrying a folder of some sort. He didn't look around, which suited me just fine. The motel parking lot was full, and my car was sandwiched between others on the road, so I hoped we had escaped his notice. Still, I couldn't shake off the uncanny feeling that he knew only too well that I was there.

Alder climbed behind the wheel. He pulled out of his space and headed for the exit.

"Follow him, but stay back," Thyme said urgently. "Don't tip him off."

I pulled out a reasonable distance behind Alder's car.

"I think he's heading for his house," Thyme said with obvious disappointment, after Alder had led us a winding ride over back roads. "Maybe we should just go back."

"I don't know," I said. Alder's car had disappeared around a sharp bend. When I drove around the curve, Alder's car was nowhere to be seen, and the road was straight for miles. I slammed on the brakes, and swerved to a stop.

"What the heck?" Thyme exclaimed.

"Where could he have gone?" I was really beginning to think Alder had mystical powers.

"I don't know, but just keep driving," Thyme said.

I did as she asked. Just up ahead was another road to the left. It was hidden by wattle trees until I was almost upon it. I turned onto it. It was paved but not as well as the main road, and my car bounced this way and that. Thyme lost some of her scrying water in the process. This road climbed rather steeply, going directly up the hill instead of winding around it. The road was narrow, so much so that if another car came, I would have to pull off to the side to allow it to pass. I fervently hoped that Alder didn't come back down the hill past us. We'd be sitting ducks.

For once, luck was on my side, because before long the road widened and the ground levelled out. Soon I saw a dirt lane down to a pretty little white house that was surrounded by bougainvillea and magnolia trees in full bloom.

"Oh gosh, how silly of me," Thyme said. "There's his car. This must be where he's living now. He sold his parents' farm after they died."

I started to pull off the road, but Thyme stopped me.

"Keep going," she said. "Don't pull over.

There's a road to the right that will take us back to town."

"Shouldn't we watch him?" I asked.

"No," Thyme said firmly, shaking her head. "It's one thing to follow him around town to find out if he has a client interested in you, but it's another thing entirely to go to his own home. A man has been murdered, after all. Do you remember the last time?"

I swerved to miss a bush turkey that had run out on the road, and then glanced at Thyme. She looked like an angry mother or a stern schoolmistress. I hoped it was because she had just lost some more scrying water, not that she was angry with me for wanting to sit outside Alder's house.

"You almost got hurt when we tried to solve Brant McCallum's murder!" she said.

I nodded. "Yes, but surely you don't think Alder Vervain had anything to do with Thomas Hale's murder?"

"Someone murdered him," Thyme said. "And it was likely someone in this town. If we're going to do help Dianne, we have to be careful."

The mood for rest of the ride home was somewhat contemplative and sombre. It wasn't until I was home that I saw that Thyme had left the small bowl of scrying water on the floor of my car. I took it inside with me and put it on the coffee table in the living room. I figured the cats wouldn't drink it, and just as well, as who knew what magical things would happen to them if they drank moon-enchanted scrying water?

After a quick dinner of chocolate ice cream and wine, I showered and dressed for bed. I wondered whether I should follow Thyme's instructions and smudge my bedroom with white sage, but then decided against it. I was way too tired for that. I was asleep almost as soon as I hit the sheets.

Later I awoke, gasping from a nightmare. I lay in bed for a moment, thinking about the bad dream. Someone had been chasing me down a long hallway that had no doors or windows. There had been footsteps behind me, and they had been getting closer.

I jumped out of bed, scattering the cats, and turned on the light. I didn't think I'd be able to go straight back to sleep, so I got a glass of water and went into the living room. I was going to look for something to watch on cable, not a horror movie of course. Willow and Hawthorn were already on the sofa, glaring at me. I reached for the remote, but then my eyes fell on the container of scrying water on the coffee table.

As I looked at it, I saw shapes forming. I blinked, at first thinking I was imagining things. I rubbed my eyes and looked again. Sure enough, I could clearly see a shadowy figure in the water. I gasped and looked more closely.

Thyme had told me that scrying came more easily to some than to others. I had assumed it wouldn't come easily to me. Yet as I peered into the depths of the dark water, I clearly saw a shadowy figure in front of my house, moving stealthily away. The sight chilled me to the bone. At the moment, I knew full well that someone had been creeping along the street outside my house in the middle of the night. And whoever it was, was filled with malicious intent towards me.

CHAPTER 11

"Don't think so hard about it." Thyme patted my shoulder as we made our way down the footpath. "You're so stressed that you're making my hair turn white!"

I shot her an apologetic smile. "Sorry."

"I'm kidding!" Thyme said with exasperation. "Come on. I know I said to be careful, but you're taking it too far. He's not a mass murderer, just a low-rate private detective. He's so great at his job that he made it obvious he was investigating you. And we don't even know yet if someone really has paid him to follow you. Even if that's true, it could just be some loser ex who can't let go."

A vivid image of my boyfriend came to mind. I remembered his scathing glares of disgust over my

Nachos of Doom. "Is that supposed to make me feel better?"

"I guess a paid stalker is hard to brush off as no big deal." It was Thyme's turn to give me an apologetic look as she shifted the basket of cream stuffed lemon cake from one arm to the other. "Sorry, Mint is better at the reassuring-people-through-a-crisis thing than I am. But if you ever want to turn anyone prematurely bald, let me know."

"There's a spell for that?" I gasped as soon as I said the words, and looked around for eavesdroppers. Luckily, no one was staring at me like I was a crazy person.

Thyme, on the other hand, seemed completely unfazed. After a quick glance around, she turned her attention back to me. "Yes, there are spells for everything. And even in a mundane way, there are herbs and oils you could put together to make it happen. But I've found that sneaking hair removal cream into their shampoo bottle tends to work faster."

I laughed. I thought for a moment that Thyme was just joking. She seemed too calm and matter of fact about it.

"Hey, it works!" Thyme waved her free hand in the air. "I have a terrible dating record. I think I have a primal need for high blood pressure and anxiety. I always end up with both a few weeks into a relationship. Payback is great stress relief—non-magical payback, that is."

"You seriously don't put Nair in their shampoo?" I didn't know whether I was amused, appalled, or just plain envious. Truth be told, I was probably envious. If I had tried to pull something like that, I bet I'd be sent to jail and I'd end up being bunked with an inmate with multiple personalities, all three of which would hate me. That would be just how my luck would roll in the revenge department.

"No I'm kidding." Thyme's mouth quirked into a grin and she ducked as I swiped at her. "I fantasise about what I'd like to do to them. Usually, it's little things like locking their keys in the car or hiding their wallet in the back of their freezer. The only thing I ever did, was to take an industrial strength magnet to my last boyfriend's memory cards."

"Memory cards?"

Thyme nodded. "On his games. A strong enough magnet can ruin a saved game. The way he played, half his life was probably on those things."

"Thyme!"

Thyme stopped walking and put her free hand on her hip. "I refuse to feel sorry for a man who throws a tantrum when a kid out-games him. He pawned my things to buy a two hundred dollar game upgrade. I don't have anything against gamers as such, but if you ever date one, make sure he's not a kleptomaniac with a Peter-Pan complex."

I was shocked. "He actually pawned your things for a game?"

"Yes, my sapphire earrings and a gold fob chain that my grandmother had given me. I did get them back in the end. Most men do make it out unscathed," Thyme assured me. "In real life, not in my mind."

We were still giggling over Thyme's ideas for revenge tactics when we arrived at *Glinda's*. Ruprecht's store was as warm and welcoming as ever. Books were shelved from top to bottom, ancient globes hung from the ceiling, and glass cabinets displayed all manner of mystical items, from crystal balls to exotic incense.

I could spend all day in *Glinda's* and still not see everything there was to see. It was a combination of a mystic library, a museum, and a set from a Harry Potter movie.

Camino waved us towards the back room. "Looks like someone is feeling better!"

Thyme grinned. "I've been giving Amelia some relationship advice on the way."

"Goddess help us!" Camino exclaimed with a shake of her head, and then glanced over at me. "Is that to say you have someone on your mind?"

"No!" I said quickly, feeling my face colour at the unexpected question.

"The handsome fire fighter perhaps?"

"No," I said again, this time truthfully. It was Alder Vervain who had come to mind, rather than Craig. I somehow couldn't bring myself to share Thyme's opinion of Alder. "Thyme was just distracting me from, well, everything."

"She has a talent for that!" Mint called from the back.

Thyme snorted rudely as she handed over the basket. "Just so you know, ignore whatever Mint's been saying about me! She's my accomplice!"

Camino laughed softly and nodded. "I'd not doubt it for a minute."

Mint peeked around the corner with a stack of small white ceramic plates in hand. "What makes you say that?"

"Don't try to play the angel, Mint." Camino

waved a knobbly finger at both Thyme and Mint. "I helped change your diapers. I likely know you two better than you know yourselves."

As the women squirmed, Camino turned her attention to me. "These two were always causing all manner of mischief when they were younger. Poor Ruprecht, trying to cope with two little bulls in his antique shop."

"We weren't that bad!" Mint insisted, her face colouring.

Thyme grinned. "Yes we were," she said with a chuckle.

"One time when Mint was about seven, she got it in her head that she was going to be a beautician when she was older. Next thing I knew, I found my poor cat, Calliope, in the kitchen sink, being dyed pink. Calliope never let Mint and Thyme near her for the rest of her days."

"Camino!" Mint was red faced as she set out the plates. "You promised not to share that silly story with guests anymore."

"Amelia isn't a guest. She's practically family," Camino sniffed, unaffected by Mint's protests.

Ruprecht shuffled out from hiding, one of his cats perched contently on his shoulder in the same way a parrot would sit on a pirate's shoulder. "And there was also your first, or should I say only, sleepover."

I dragged my eyes away from the cat on his shoulder and asked, "What happened?"

"We decided to paint," Thyme said simply. "We painted a Ming Vase, a Victorian statue, and a jade dragon. We were terrors. It wasn't until high school that Mint decided her life's goal was to be boring."

"I am not boring!" Mint protested. "Last week I went line dancing."

"Line dancing?" I said without thinking.

"I had a really nice time," Mint said defensively as she busied herself cutting the cake.

"Dancing?" Thyme appeared to be dubious at the claim.

"It was a nice time. I even talked with a man from out of town."

I noticed Ruprecht and Camino exchanging a look of surprise. This was apparently news to them.

"While dancing?"

"No, Thyme! I didn't dance. Happy?" Mint huffed and scratched her arm. "I break out in hives when I'm totally surrounded. Sue me!"

I was relieved that none of my embarrassing childhood stories would ever come to light. They would never let me live them down.

"I apologise, Amelia." Ruprecht reached out to pat my hand. "We're getting away from ourselves. The whole point of the evening was to help you with your problem. Is there anything we can do?"

Suddenly, the reality of the whole thing came crashing back—the body on the porch, and Alder Vervain's claim that someone had hired him to investigate my possible involvement in the matter.

I plastered what I hoped was a cheerful and reassuring look on my face. "Oh well, what can I do? Hopefully, the police will solve the murder soon, and find out what the man was doing at my house."

No one seemed convinced. Thankfully, they didn't try to press the matter but instead helped themselves to the lemon cake. It was Thyme's creation of course. I was barely able to make lemonade unsupervised, let alone a cake.

Thyme seemed appeased at the explanation. "How are you sleeping? Would you like me to stay over tonight, and Mint too?"

"No!" Camino and Ruprecht exclaimed in unison. The harmony of their tone and expression hinted that they had years of experience shutting down sleepovers after the Ming Vase incident.

I shook my head. "Thanks, but I'm okay."

"The house did feel a little extra temperamental

the last time I was there," Mint said. "I imagine it wasn't too happy having someone die on its porch."

"Trust me, I feel the same way."

"Now to business," Ruprecht said. "Thyme tells me she's filled you in about Alder Vervain."

"Even his name is a mockery!" Camino snapped.

I was puzzled. "What do you mean? He can't help his name."

Ruprecht shook his head. "To the contrary, my dear, that is not his birth name. He legally changed it some years ago. He was born as Tommy Hopkins."

I nearly choked on my lemon cake. "Tommy Hopkins? He doesn't look like a Tommy Hopkins at all. Surely it doesn't matter that he changed his name, though?"

"It's the context, Amelia," Camino said stiffly. "Those of us who are hereditary kitchen witches in this town have names of herbs that are important to magical practices. Alder is from a long line of people strenuously opposed to witches, and so he changed his name to herbs."

I was beginning to catch on. "So you think he changed his name to a kitchen witch name to mock you?"

"Yes!" everyone exclaimed in unison.

"Alder is a strongly protective herb," Camino explained. "Both its roots and leaves offer powerful protection from enemies. It undoes jinxes, too."

"And vervain?"

"You probably know it as verbena," Camino said.

I didn't, but I nodded anyway. Clearly I had a long way to go in my witch education.

"Vervain is also used against evil and to break a jinx. It was one of nine herbs traditionally used in European witchcraft as a protection against witches."

"That's right, Camino," Ruprecht said. "So, Amelia, you can see that Alder Vervain's name is ironic. He chose to name himself after two herbs that offer protection, and one of those herbs offers protection specifically against witches."

I suppose I could see their point, but Alder didn't strike me as someone who would do such a thing. Still, I was a new witch and I had to defer to their judgment. "Okay, so I know mint is used to draw and protect money, and break curses, too. Thyme is used in the same way, to protect and attract money."

Camino nodded. "Well done. Thyme also stops nightmares, if it's burned before you go to bed."

I wish I'd known that earlier, I thought. Aloud I said, "But what sort of herb is camino? I've never heard of it before."

Thyme chimed in. "It's one of the most important herbs there is. Abre camino, also known as Road Opener."

"Its botanical name is Eupatorium villosum," Ruprecht said. "Well, these days it's known as Koanophyllon villosum. I'll go and get the mother bottle of Road Opener oil. Wait here."

He soon returned with a large bottle. It was clear. The liquid inside was murky brown and appeared to have thick stalks floating in it. "It's all but impossible to buy the plant in Australia," Ruprecht said. "I managed to buy some seeds from overseas years ago, and I grow several plants in my greenhouse."

"The seeds went through customs all right?" I asked with surprise.

"Yes, it's Road Opener after all," Ruprecht said with a chuckle. "It opens the way, removes obstacles, stuff like that."

"What about your name?" I asked. "What kind of herb is a ruprecht?"

Everyone dissolved into helpless peals of laughter, while my face flushed red.

Ruprecht was the first to regain his composure. "Ruprecht isn't a herb, but my middle name is Celery."

I did my best not to laugh. "Celery?" I asked, wondering if I had heard correctly. "The stuff you eat in salads?"

Ruprecht nodded solemnly. "Celery increases psychic abilities and helps people have prophetic dreams. You can put the seeds under your pillow, or burn them on charcoal."

"Oh," was all I could manage.

"At any rate," Ruprecht continued, "I pulled a tarot card just before you all came here today. It was The Fool, reversed."

Everyone looked at each other. Even I knew that meant injustice, poor choices, even madness. Were they right about Alder Vervain?

CHAPTER 12

$\mathcal{I}$ unlocked the front door and flipped over the sign to 'Open,' despite the fact it was half an hour before opening time. With everything that had been going on, all I wanted was one day of peace and normalcy. Surely that was not too much to ask?

I walked over to the front counter and began looking through the previous and current orders. I couldn't cook, but I could make sure that the business side of things was in order. That much I could do. I soon became engrossed in analysing the numbers. In fact, I was so engrossed, that I barely noticed when the door opened and what I assumed was my first customer for the day walked in.

However, it was the two detectives. "We would

like you to assist us in our investigation," Detective Harrison said formally.

My chest tightened as I struggled to make sense of what was going on. "I'm sorry, but I don't think I understand. I don't know anything at all. I just discovered the body."

"That is not something we can discuss here," Detective Sassafras said. "Would you be willing to accompany us back to the station?"

"Am I in trouble? Should I call a friend so someone knows where I am?"

Harrison shook his head. "That won't be necessary, Miss Spelled. We just want you to help us with our inquiries."

Clearly I had no option but to go with them. I nodded in defeat. "I just need to leave a note for my employee," I said. I scrawled a note, and then took it to the kitchen where Thyme was sure to see it. I grabbed my handbag and keys and then followed the officers out of the store, flipping the sign back over and locking up before I left.

"The station isn't far from here, so you can ride with us," Sassafras said.

I wasn't sure how to respond. It wasn't an order, although it didn't sound too much like a request. I wasn't being arrested, but it sure felt that way.

"Okay," I said. As soon as I set foot on the street, the rain came down harder. Clearly this wasn't my day. People on the street stopped to stare when they saw me with the two men, who looked even more like detectives than the ones on TV. I felt awful.

Sassafras opened the door for me to get in. I crawled into the back of the vehicle and the door slammed shut behind me.

"Okay then, let's get this over with so you can get back to your shop," Detective Harrison said, as soon as we arrived.

I followed them into the police station, where everyone in the waiting room turned to stare at me. I was soaked and my shoes squelched with every step. I felt I would just die of embarrassment.

Detective Sassafras pointed towards the end of a long corridor. "The interview room is right at the end of this hall." He walked ahead, leaving me to walk with Harrison.

Harrison turned to me. "Just tell the truth."

"I don't have anything to hide!" I said in alarm.

"Just tell us the truth and you'll have nothing to fear," he said.

When we got to the room, Harrison waved me inside. "Take a seat. We'll be right in to talk to you." He closed the door behind him.

I looked around the room. Should I have asked for a lawyer? Why wasn't there a one-way mirror on the wall like on TV shows? Was that camera on the wall recording me sitting there? Were they out there watching me to see what I would do? Did they really think I had something to do with Thomas Hale's murder?

I shook my head. This was no time to let my imagination run away with me. I looked instead at the worn furniture. The wooden-topped table looked ancient, as did the wooden chairs. Black stuff was peeling off the metal legs. Surely they could afford something better than this. The walls were brick and painted in the most horrible shade of pale green I had ever seen.

I debated whether to take off my rain-filled shoes and empty them out on the floor, but finally decided not to. If they were in fact watching me, it might make them mad.

Finally, the door swung open. Harrison walked in, holding a thin folder that he threw on the table. He was followed by Sassafras, who said nothing as he took a seat opposite me. Both men looked solemn.

Harrison remained standing. He opened the file and jabbed his finger on the front page. "This is your statement," he said sternly. "You told us that you had never met Thomas Hale. In fact, you alleged that you had never seen him. Is that correct?"

"Yes," I said, wondering what was going on.

Harrison sat down, and then bodily dragged his chair across to the table in one motion. It made a horrible scraping sound, and at that moment, one of the florescent light panels started to flicker in a most irritating manner.

Harrison flipped over a page or two, pulled out some large photos, and skimmed them across the table in front of me.

At first glance, I wasn't quite sure what I was seeing. To my horror, they were photos of me with the victim. "What's going on?"

The cop leant closer and separated the photos. He laid them out individually, and pointed at each one as he kept his eyes locked on mine. "Can you explain to us how we have several photos of you with Thomas Hale, a man you claimed never to have met?" His tone was accusatory.

I swallowed the large lump in my throat. My hands trembled, and I sat there at a loss for words. "That's not me," I said after an interval. I held it up to my face to get a better look. "I know it looks like me, but it isn't," I said in a small voice. "It can't be."

Harrison scratched his chin, and then leant back in his chair. "So you're claiming you have a look-alike are, you?" he said sarcastically. "A doppelganger?"

I stared at the photos. "Okay, it does look like me, but the photographs must have been faked or something."

"Faked?" the second cop chimed in. He shook his head, clearly not believing a word I said. "They look pretty convincing to me."

"Haven't you ever heard of Photoshop?" I shot back.

Harrison glared at me. "So, now you're saying someone is framing you for this? First, a body shows up at your front door and you claim he's a complete stranger. Secondly, we receive photos in the mail that show you and the victim together. So why don't you tell us why someone would go through all that trouble?"

I sighed. They didn't believe me at all, and part of me didn't blame them. I probably wouldn't believe my story either if I were one of them. "I know it sounds crazy, but I've never met that man before in my life. My only explanation is that someone's trying to frame me. I bet those photos were sent to you anonymously."

The two cops exchanged a look, and then Harrison handed the file to Sassafras. He stood up abruptly and walked out of the room, slamming the door behind him.

"Do you have diabetes?" Harrison asked.

"No!" I said. I knew where this was going. Word was that insulin had killed Hale.

"Do you know anyone with diabetes?"

"No, not a soul," I said truthfully.

"All right, this is what's going to happen," Harrison said. "Those photographs will be submitted to the Forensics Imaging team for analysis. If they determine that they were indeed doctored, then you'll be dropped as a person of interest and we'll be one step closer to finding the real killer."

Relief finally washed over me. "So, does that mean I can go now?"

The cop opened the door and turned back to me. "Yes," he said, nodding. "But you had better not be lying to us."

CHAPTER 13

"Come into the back room. I think I'm in some serious hot water," I said to Thyme as soon as I got back to the shop. Luckily, there were no customers at the time.

Thyme's face was filled with anxiety. "What happened with the police? I've been worried sick since I saw your note. And you're soaked!"

"I'm completely spooked, to be honest," I said. "They had a whole bunch of photos that showed me with the victim."

Thyme gasped. "With Thomas Hale?" She handed me a towel.

I nodded. "The police got some photos in the mail that show me with Thomas Hale—when he was alive, obviously. I don't mean with me finding his body. Anyway, as you know, I've never seen the guy before. The day I found him lying on my front porch was the first day I had ever seen him."

"I wonder why someone would do that? First, the body turned up where it had no place to be, and now you're showing up in photos where you have no place to be. It's rather peculiar."

I agreed. "It sure is. The good news is that the police sent the photos to the forensic lab to be examined. Obviously, they'll find out that they're Photoshopped or something."

"Then you have nothing to worry about," Thyme said.

I chewed one fingernail. "That's not what I'm worried about," I said. "It would be pretty bad if the police forensics lab couldn't tell when images are Photoshopped. What's really worrying me is that someone's trying to frame me!" My voice rose to a high pitch.

"Alder Vervain," Thyme said at once.

I shook my head. "No, I don't think it's him." *I hope it's not him*, I added silently.

"Well, who then?" Thyme asked. "It fits with the pattern of what his family always did."

"Maybe it's the person who paid him to follow me. Maybe that person is the murderer, and they paid him to take photos of me so they could Photoshop them onto the victim's photos," I said. I thought that was clever of me, but Thyme looked sceptical.

"That's a bit of a stretch, isn't it? And we really don't know if anyone has employed him to watch you, or whether he just made that up."

I shrugged. "No, not really. Whoever sent those photos to the cop is obviously trying to frame me."

"Well, we can't let that happen then, can we?" Thyme said. "I'm going to cast a spell."

"A spell?"

Thyme nodded. "A spell to speed up the forensic tests and prove that you had nothing to do with it. Do you mind if we put a 'Back in ten minutes' sign on the door?"

"No, that's fine. We don't get many customers on a rainy day, anyway." I hurried off to do as she asked.

When I returned, Thyme was in the process of placing dishes on the floor. "Hey, see those four dishes?" she said, putting the last one down. "Put one candle on each and light them."

I proceeded to do as she said. "What happens next?"

"This is called a circle of protection. Some witches, before they cast a spell, protect the area from harmful and negative energies," Thyme explained, walking to the centre of the candles. She then pointed at each one as she continued. "These candles each represent one of the elements, as well as each of the cardinal points. We'll use them to call the quarters."

"Oh," I said. "Is this really going to work? The forensic team will just randomly get the results faster? And I've been reading up on witches. Isn't casting a circle a Wiccan thing, but you're traditional witches, not Wiccan?"

"There are no rules, really," Thyme explained. "Traditional witches are usually eclectic. We borrow a bit here, a bit there. Ruprecht doesn't cast a circle, but I like to, because it helps me focus. Sometimes I don't, though."

"Oh," I said. "Sorry to ask. I'm still fairly new to this."

"We were all new once upon a time," Thyme replied, "and questions are good. Ask as many questions as you like." She turned to the first of the four candles. "I ask that the God and Goddess bless this circle so that I may be free and protected within this space. So mote it be," she said, spinning and pointing her arms around the circle. "Now I'm going to call the quarters."

I was lost in my own thoughts for a moment or two, but then focused on Thyme as she went through all four elements. "Guardians of the North, element of earth, I call upon you to be present during this ritual," she said. "Amelia, please pass me some of that coffee."

I fetched it for her and placed it in her hand, making sure not to step out of the circle. "Here you go. So coffee speeds up spells?" I asked.

Thyme nodded. "I'm adding it to this spell. See, this is a yellow candle for communication."

I then stood quietly, watching Thyme.

"Spirits and guides, I ask you now for swiftness," she said. "We seek for the authorities to hurry and find out that the photos of Amelia were Photoshopped. I thank and release you now!"

I looked around the room, and at the same time I could feel a strange sensation all around me. The flames on the candles momentarily flared. At that moment I felt sure that the spell would work—I just wasn't sure exactly how it would work.

I smiled as a feeling of hope washed over me. Maybe now things would get sorted out and the police would believe me. Other than a few altered photographs and the corpse on my porch, the cops had no reason to think I was involved in Thomas Hale's death.

The spell was over and Thyme had closed the circle. "Okay, all done," she announced. "We should be hearing from the police sometime soon."

"So how exactly is this spell going to work? How will it affect the people doing the forensic tests?"

Thyme smiled. "The worst thing we can do is to try to figure out *how* a spell is going to work. I asked that the police would quickly get the results that the photos were faked. The spell was to speed things up. How that plays out is rather irrelevant. Don't even think about it. Now we'd better hurry and open the shop."

CHAPTER 14

"They've put onion in it again," I complained bitterly. "I clearly told them that onion makes me sick." I tossed the whole salad into the garbage.

"Couldn't you have just picked the onion off the top?" Thyme asked me.

I shook my head. "No. I get sick if I eat anything that onion's touched. Well, that only leaves the beet fritters."

After my trying day, I'd invited Thyme home for dinner. Obviously, I wasn't going to cook, so I'd bought take out for us at the Middle Pub on the way home.

Bayberry Creek was a three pub town. In Australia, towns are often categorised by their number of pubs, an Aussie pub being a combination of hotel, bar and often a restaurant. All three pubs in Bayberry Creek served good food, but the menu at the Middle Pub was my favourite. They just seemed to be a little overly fond of onion.

The TV suddenly turned on by itself.

Thyme let out a squeal. "How did that happen?" she asked.

I groaned. "It's the house. It's become obsessed with watching Mixed Martial Arts tournaments and a whole lot of old martial arts movies—you know, *Kill Bill*, *Seven Samurai*, or anything with Bruce Lee, Jackie Chan, Steven Seagal, Jean-Claude Van Damme, Cynthia Rothrock and all those actors. Sometimes I'm in the middle of watching a good movie and the house suddenly changes the channel. To tell you the truth, I've given up, and I end up watching those movies with the house." I realised how strange that sounded as soon as I said it, but if anyone would understand, it would be Thyme.

In fact, after several attempts to watch *The Notebook* with the house changing the channel every few minutes, we finally gave up and watched *Enter the Dragon*.

We had just finished our meals when there was a loud knock on the front door. I exchanged glances with Thyme. "Who could it be?"

"Answer it and you'll find out," Thyme said smugly. "I'll take these plates to the kitchen."

I rolled my eyes and hurried down the long hallway of the house, dodging Willow and Hawthorn as I went. Why do cats always try to trip you up when you're in a hurry?

I could see the silhouettes of two people through the stained glass panels of the old doorway. It was hard to tell if they were male or female through the pink and green glass.

As I reached for the brass doorknob, I peered through the glass panes, wondering if more bad news was about to be delivered to me.

I opened the door with my heart in my mouth. Standing there were the two detectives, Harrison and Sassafras.

"May we come in?" Harrison asked.

They weren't holding handcuffs, which I took as a good sign. Harrison was holding a folder. I wondered if he went anywhere without it. After a moment of staring at them with my mouth open, I opened the screen door and let them in. They followed me into the living room.

Thyme hurried into the room. "Is everything all right?"

Harrison simply glanced at me as he opened his

folder. He threw some photos onto the coffee table. They slid across and stopped just short of going over the edge. "These are the photos of you and the victim that we were sent."

I raised my eyebrows at Thyme, but she simply shrugged. The detective's tone was accusatory. Had they found out that I was telling the truth, or did they actually think that the doctored images were real now? Panic set in as my breathing became laboured.

"You don't have the results back from forensics already, do you?" I asked him.

When Harrison shook his head, my heart sank. "No, one of the uniformed officers who is a keen photographer had a look at the photos." He leant over and picked up one of the photos, and then held it up as if he were making a presentation. "If you pay close attention to the edges of your image in the photos, there's an imbalance with the lighting. It's hard to see if you don't know what you're looking for. They have been doctored."

I breathed a big sigh of relief. "Does that mean you believe me now?"

"We have to wait for forensics to give us the official word," Harrison said, "but for the purposes of our investigation, we now know that those photos are fake."

"And that means that we think someone altered those photographs for a reason," Sassafras said, his eyes narrowed.

"Of course they did it for a reason," Thyme interjected, glaring at the cop. "Someone's trying to frame Amelia. Can't you see that?"

"The evidence does suggest that someone is trying to frame Miss Spelled, but who would want to do that?" Harrison asked, focusing his gaze on me. "And how did they get photos of you?"

"I really don't have a clue," I said. "None of this makes any sense to me!"

"Oh come on," Sassafras shot back. "If you expect us to believe that someone is trying to frame you for murder, you should be able to name at least one person that would want to do such a thing. Are you saying you don't know a single person with a motive to bring harm your way?"

"No!" I said. "I'm the victim in this and I don't appreciate being treated as a criminal. I don't know why anyone would do this, but someone has!"

"Yes, someone who also has access to photos of you," Harrison added.

"Maybe this person killed Thomas Hale and

just wanted to pin it on the first scapegoat that they were able to find," Thyme said. "Perhaps they only chose Amelia because the body was found on her porch."

Harrison put his hands on his hips. "We aren't saying that suspicion is still focused on you," he said, staring at me, "but until we know exactly what's going on and who's behind it, we need to investigate every possible avenue."

I sighed and looked over at Thyme. She didn't appear any happier with the officer's response than I was.

"I still think you have to have some type of idea who would do this to you though, in all honesty," Harrison continued. "It would help if you could give us a name. Do you have any enemies? Who would want to do you harm? Maybe an ex-boyfriend? A disgruntled business associate? An unhappy customer?"

"I really can't think of anyone," I said. I had sent my ex-boyfriend to the hospital with food poisoning, entirely by accident of course, but he was hardly likely to kill someone just to frame me for murder. He was upset, but he wasn't that upset.

LATER THAT NIGHT, after Thyme had left, I decided to try a spell of my own. According to my notes, vanilla and sugar were added to spells to make people well disposed to the spellcaster. I sure needed that. The cops were no doubt still somewhat suspicious of me, and Kayleen shook her fist at me every time she saw me. That morning, I had even gone to the Post Office to pay for a Post Office box and a mail redirect from my home address to the box. I was irritated that I'd had to go to that length and expense just because my mail lady had a personality disorder.

I assembled the items for the sweetening spell: self-lighting charcoal disks for burning incense, as well as sugar, vanilla, honey, and clove buds for friendship, and rosemary for happiness.

I stood in my kitchen and wondered what to do next. I wasn't going to cast a circle. After all, Thyme had said that it wasn't necessary for traditional witches, and I was a traditional kitchen witch. At any rate, I wasn't sure I would do it correctly.

I wrote my intent on a piece of paper: 'Everyone around me is happy.'

I got my ovenproof dish and set it in the middle of the table. I half filled it with sugar, and then drizzled honey around the edges. Everything I'd read said that honey and sugar were used in sweetening spells. I put clove buds as well as sprigs of rosemary from the garden on top of the sugar. Next to the dish, I placed my small cauldron. It had been my aunt's. I put sugar in the cauldron.

I fetched the bottles of self-lighting incense. I had sandalwood, basil, pennyroyal and rosemary. One of the books in the house's library stated that these were the ingredients for 'happy home incense.' I mixed them in a small dish.

I had also learned that birthday candles are ideal for a quick spell. I shoved the birthday candle down into the sugar, and luckily, it stood upright.

Now to start. I took a deep breath and lit the birthday candle. I picked up a charcoal disk with tongs, and held it over the flame. It fizzled and sparkled for a while, and when it stopped, I dropped it into the cauldron. I then grabbed a handful of the happy home incense and dropped it in the cauldron as well. At once, it produced thick white smoke, which quickly filled the room.

I turned my attention to the birthday candle, but it had already burned down to the level of the sugar. At that moment, the sugar burst into flames. My studies had indicated that sudden flames were a good sign that the spell was being fulfilled, so I didn't know whether to be pleased or alarmed. The decision was made for me when the flames reached the ceiling.

I grabbed the first thing I saw, the self-lighting incense, and threw it on the flames to douse them. It had the opposite effect. By the time I'd filled a bowl with water and thrown it on the flames, the kitchen was filled with smoke. The smoke detectors screeched.

I ran into the hallway to get some fresh air, and saw the silhouette of someone outside the front door. No doubt I hadn't been able to hear the knocking over the crackle of the flames.

I hurried down the corridor and opened the door. It was Camino. She handed me a gift-wrapped box. "A small gift for you, dear. I've noticed you only have those flimsy pyjamas."

"Come in," I said, and shut the door behind her.

We walked into the living room and I at once unwrapped the gift. It was a koala onesie with over-sized matching koala slippers. "Oh thank you, you delightful, wonderful woman," I gushed, throwing my arms around Camino and hugging her.

"You're so welcome, dear," she said. "And what lovely white smoke filling the room. How pretty it is as it makes it way around and around." She giggled and clapped her hands with delight.

I smiled at Willow and Hawthorn who were purring loudly and rolling around the floor.

I hugged Camino again. "It's wonderful to see you!" I exclaimed. "I haven't seen you for hours."

Camino smiled. "Amelia, you've done a spell! How clever of you, you adorable girl."

I beamed. "Thank you for your compliment, dear woman. It was a sweetening spell."

"I thought as much," Camino said. "I wondered why the house was purring."

"Oh, I thought that was just thunder," I said. "What a wonderful sound!"

Camino hurried to the windows. "Let's open all the windows in the house and get this smoke out. There's only so much sweetness one can take."

CHAPTER 15

J looked up from the front counter as the door chimed. I was placing four cupcakes in a white cardboard box for Mrs Smythe, an elderly woman who came in once a week and always purchased the same thing, four vanilla cupcakes with pink strawberry icing. My breath caught in my throat as I saw who had just walked in. Craig.

I'd had a crush on Craig since I'd moved to town, but that had waned somewhat since I'd met Alder Vervain. I thought there was chemistry with Alder, and not so much with Craig, but was that just because Alder was mysterious? The mysterious—and possibly witch-hating criminal, if Thyme was right—Alder, versus the good, wholesome fire fighter Craig.

I placed Mrs Smythe's order on the counter, and then took the payment. It was exactly the right amount, down to the change. Some customers handed me fifty dollars for a four dollar cupcake. If only all customers were like Mrs Smythe. She thanked me, took her box, and turned for the door. Craig stepped back with her, and held the door open for her. When she was outside, he returned.

"Hey," he said with a smile.

"Hey," I replied, doing my best to sound cool and normal, and most likely failing. "Do you need a cupcake?"

"I always need a cupcake, but I came to ask you something," Craig said.

"What's up?"

"Will you have lunch with me today?"

I wasn't sure I had heard him correctly. "Sorry?"

Craig grinned, an easy, lopsided smile. "I was wondering if you wanted to come out with me for lunch. I was thinking… Oh well, I don't know. It's probably stupid, probably not your thing…" His voice trailed off.

"No, it's totally my thing," I said hurriedly. I'd had a crush on the man for ages, and just because I had recently taken a weird liking to a potentially dangerous man didn't mean I shouldn't give Craig a chance. No, in fact that was even more reason why I should give Craig a chance.

"Well," Craig said, "what time do you go to lunch?"

I could tell he was somewhat embarrassed. "Around twelve, usually," I said. "If that suits you?"

Craig nodded. "I'll see you then." His face flushed red, which I thought was cute. He turned and left.

I then noticed Thyme standing in the doorway. She was using her hip to hold open the door that separated the back kitchen and the showroom floor. "I knew it," she said.

"Knew what?"

Thyme came forward, swinging her hips as she did so, dancing around me. "He loves you! He loves you!" she sang in the most irritating fashion.

I laughed and shook my head. "Settle down! Stop that!"

That only seemed to spur her on. "He loves you!" she sang, more loudly this time.

"Shut up!" I said, pushing her away. "He doesn't!"

"Maybe you'll get your chance today," Thyme

snickered. "All I'm saying is that you and this guy are in love."

"Shut it. Get back to work," I said in a fake stern voice.

Thyme giggled and returned to the kitchen.

I rolled my eyes. "What, are we back at school now?" I said to the empty shop.

The morning seemed to drag on, and it was as if all the irritating customers had come at once. There was a woman with three children under five, three of the most undisciplined, wild children I had ever seen. They had put their sticky fingers all over the glass display fronts. Their mother hadn't noticed—or perhaps she had, and simply didn't care. As they were leaving, the three children had a cupcake fight right in my store.

I was on my hands and knees, scrubbing globs of icing and half-chewed cupcake off the floor, when the next customer had come in. This one was irate, and had demanded her money back on a sponge cake. I excused myself to wash my hands, and when I returned to the counter, saw that she had removed the cake from its box. It had a large mouthful out of one side. "It's vanilla!" she had screeched at me. "I asked for caramel! I want my money back!"

I checked the order book, and sure enough, there were the words, 'Mrs Hall: vanilla sponge cake' right next to her signature. Still, the customer is always right, so I gave her back her money. She stormed out of the shop.

I had been examining the bite mark, wondering if the woman had a werewolf in her family—who would know? It was Bayberry Creek after all—when the next customer had come in. This one had demanded a refund because her cake was stale. She had bought it the previous week.

Okay, I admit I'd lost it by the next customer. I was standing behind the counter, and a red-faced man rushed in. "Do you work here, love?" he asked.

"No," said. "I'm a supermodel just doing a photo shoot."

He called me a few fancy names and then left even faster than he'd come in.

By then, I was wondering what job I could do if I sold the cake shop. I thought of some options, and none of them included retail.

Thankfully, there were no more customers for a while, and so there was time for my nerves to turn to jelly. The last half hour before Craig arrived seemed to drag on forever.

And, finally, there he was. Craig had always

been cute. Well, more than cute actually—he was handsome. For once, he wasn't in his fire fighter uniform, and he looked just as good in his street clothes.

"Ready?" he asked. He was holding a bunch of flowers. They looked like wildflowers, as though he had picked them straight from a beautiful meadow of which only he knew the location, because as he frequently proved, he was the perfect man. Or at least it seemed like he might be to me, but in fairness, I hadn't exactly spent much time with him. But still, in my fantasy life in my head, he was perfect. I felt like I was in a cheesy romance movie. "These are for you," he said, stating the obvious.

"Oh, wow," I said. "I don't think anyone has ever brought me flowers before."

Craig grinned. "Well, now someone has."

I reached forward and took the flowers. "Just give me a minute to put them in something." I turned and hurried into the kitchen, but Thyme immediately snatched the flowers from me and pushed me back out the swinging doors. "Have fun!" she said. "I'll put these in water."

Craig was waiting at the front door, and he held it open for me. He led me to his SUV, a big black thing that suited him perfectly. He even held the door open for me as I climbed into the large car. He closed the door and hurried around to the driver's side. The engine roared to life, and Craig floored it. I was all but flung back in my seat. He drove two blocks, and then we pulled over.

I had the urge to say, "Why didn't we walk?" but I thought the better of it. I had a bad track record with dating, so perhaps I should do the opposite of what I had done in the past—at least to some degree.

He had stopped outside Rewards Café, a place I usually avoided. For a start, the name was ironic. Also, they were so slow that once I'd had to wait over half an hour for a take out soy latte and a tomato toastie, and I was the only customer there at the time. To add insult to injury, the latte was so weak that I'd thrown it out. I don't like strong coffee, but I do like to be able to taste it.

I also had an uncomfortable thought. Rewards Café was by far the cheapest place to eat, probably because none of the locals frequented the place. I thought back to the wildflowers. Was Craig a cheapskate? No, surely not. I shook my head and silently scolded myself. I was just looking for faults.

Craig led the way to the seating area in the garden. I sat in the only available shady spot, under a spreading lilac tree. It dropped bits of blossom on me every time a breeze came up, but I didn't mind. That was preferable to sitting out in the sun.

Craig handed me the menu with a flourish. There were burgers, sandwiches, salads, and quiches to choose from. I chose a soy latte and a big garden salad with no onion. I stressed that part to Craig. I still wasn't sure who was paying, so I reached for my handbag.

Craig patted my hand. "My treat," he said, before disappearing inside to order and leaving me to contend with the blowflies.

I would have preferred to sit inside. It was cool in there, and the surroundings were pleasant, nicely polished floorboards and charming chalk-painted tables. However, the outside eating area featured mismatched iron tables and uncomfortable wooden chairs scattered randomly over what looked like an old parking area.

Stop being so critical, I scolded myself, as I shooed a particularly large blowfly with the plastic menu.

Finally, Craig returned, and we had the chance to talk. I had been looking forward to this since I had arrived in town. Yet it did not quite meet my expectations. Craig talked the whole time about himself, and never once asked me anything about myself.

During a particularly long dissertation about Craig's childhood, I wiped a lilac blossom out of my hair and looked around aimlessly at the other patrons. To my shock, I saw Alder Vervain sitting at a table across from us. He was close enough to hear what we said. When had he arrived?

"Are you all right?" Craig asked. "You look like you've seen a ghost."

I realised I must have gasped. "Oh, it's just the time," I said. "I should be getting back to the shop so Thyme can go to lunch." I stood up, and at that moment, Alder and I locked eyes.

Fortunately, Craig stood up too, blocking my view of Alder. I followed Craig out of the café after shooting a glare at Alder on my way. I was cross. It was taking it too far to follow me when I was on a date. And how dare he sit so close that he could hear what we said! I shook my head. The nerve of the man!

"How about tomorrow?"

"Oh, sorry?" Craig had pulled to a stop outside my store. In my anger with Alder, I hadn't realised that Craig had been speaking. "Tomorrow?"

Craig smiled at me and cut the engine. "I asked

if you would like to come to dinner with me tomorrow night."

I nodded. "I'd love to," I said, "and thanks for lunch."

I was about to get out of the car when Craig leant over and pressed his lips to mine. I pulled away before he had much of a chance to do anything. I didn't want to kiss him for the first time on a first date, and certainly not in a car.

Craig pulled away with a roar of the engine, waving out the window and blasting the horn.

CHAPTER 16

*a*s soon as I returned from lunch with Craig, I was busy tackling customers, cleaning, and doing paperwork. *Oh, the joys of owning your own store*, I thought.

"Here are the cakes that Mr Sanders ordered," Thyme said, emerging from the kitchen with several boxes in her arms. She placed them in a neat pile on top of the counter. "We've been so busy that you haven't told me how it was."

I was puzzled. "How what was?"

"Don't you what was me!" she shot back. "Are you going to stand there and act like nothing happened between you and Craig today?"

"Oh!" I said with a laugh. "For a minute I didn't know what on earth you were talking about."

Thyme walked over to me and put her hands on her hips. "Well, now that you do, spill it!"

"It's not that big of a deal," I said, my cheeks warming with embarrassment.

"So, did he ask you out again?"

I nodded. "We're just going out to dinner, that's all."

"That's all? Do you at least know where he's taking you? Or what you're going to wear?" Thyme seemed more excited than I was.

"I love your enthusiasm, but calm down," I said. I would have said more, but the jingle of the front door opening interrupted us.

Dianne walked in. "Hi, you two," she said.

"How have you been?" Thyme asked her.

Dianne crouched in front of the display case and slowly pointed to each pastry in turn. "Madam Dianne has been okay, but it would be much better if the police would stop snooping around my shop."

"Are they still bothering you?" I asked with dismay.

"From time to time," she said. "They treat me like a suspect and it's rather annoying. I mean, seriously, why would I want to hurt that man?"

"Why would anyone?" Thyme asked. "That's

the million dollar question." Just then, the oven timer sounded and she hurried back to the kitchen.

I sighed. "I'm sure this will all blow over soon enough. They've even taken me in for questioning."

Dianne looked up from the pastries with interest. "They did? Why? What did they say?"

I rubbed my temples. "Someone anonymously sent them some photographs of me with the victim. Luckily, the police found out they were faked."

"They were faked?" she parroted. She looked thoughtful for a moment, and then turned her attention to the cupcakes. "Are those red velvet cupcakes low-fat?"

"Sure are," I said. "All the cupcakes in that display case there are low-fat, but the double chocolate cupcakes aren't."

Dianne nodded. "I'll have two double chocolate cupcakes, then."

I leant down behind the display case to retrieve the cupcakes. As I stood up and placed the box on the countertop, the two detectives walked in.

There were staring at Dianne, which annoyed me. "Is there something I can help you with?" I asked.

"We'd like to speak to you in private, Ms

Spelled," Detective Sassafras said, looking directly at Dianne.

"You can speak in front of Dianne," I said. "She's a friend."

"Is that so?" Harrison said. He and Sassafras exchanged glances. "All right, as you wish." He held up a sealed plastic bag. It had a large, white label on it and inside the bag was an old, weathered wallet. "Have you seen this wallet before?"

I stared at the wallet. "I don't believe so," I said. "Should it look familiar or something?"

"That's what I am asking you," he replied. "We found it in your garbage, after all."

"You found what in the garbage?" Thyme asked, appearing from the kitchen. "What's going on? And don't you need a warrant for that?"

"No, because the garbage was on public property," Sassafras said. "Once you put out the garbage for the garbage trucks to collect, it becomes the property of the town, giving us full jurisdiction over its contents."

"Okay, but how is an old wallet relevant to anything? Perhaps a customer left it here in the shop and somehow it found its way into the bin. These things happen," I said.

"It's not just any wallet," Harrison explained.

"It belonged to the victim. It wasn't on his body, and it wasn't near your porch. It was in your garbage can, your home garbage can, that is, not your shop's. We'd like you to come back to the station to answer a few questions."

"I can't see why that matters," I said. "The poor man was murdered at my house! Whoever murdered him obviously threw his wallet into my garbage."

"I'm afraid it's not quite that simple, Ms Spelled," Harrison said solemnly. "If you will accompany us down to the station, we can discuss the matter further."

Once more, I followed the police out of my store. From the back seat of their vehicle, I watched my store slowly disappear.

After a short drive, we arrived at the Bayberry Creek Police Station and parked close to the building. The officers got out of the car and then Harrison opened the back door for me. "Please follow us," Sassafras said sternly.

I walked behind the two cops as they went through a back door with a sign declaring it was off-limits to non-employee persons. We headed down a long, dark corridor.

Harrison looked over at me. "We usually only

bring detainees in this way, but the cells are empty right now."

"The cells?" I asked. I looked around, wondering if they had brought me past the jail cells just to frighten me.

This time, they showed me into a different interview room. It had a large metal table with a metal chair on one side and two comfortable looking, upholstered chairs opposite it. The walls were a faded shade of beige.

"Have a seat," Sassafras barked, pointing to the lone metal chair.

The three of us sat down. Harrison, as usual, had a folder. He pushed the folder towards me and then opened it up, revealing a photo of me sitting by the local creek.

"How did you get that photo?" I asked.

"Don't you want to know what the murder victim was doing with it?" Sassafras asked.

"What?" My heart sank to my stomach. "Someone planted photos of me in his wallet, too?"

"I'm sure that's what you'd like us to believe," he said, glaring at me.

Harrison leant forward. "If you're not being honest with us, that makes it so much more difficult —for us, and for you."

"But I'm not lying," I insisted. "You already know that someone faked photos of me with the victim and sent them to you. It's obvious that someone's trying to frame me. Can't you see that?" I just wanted to scream. This was just ridiculous.

The cops appeared unmoved. "We have an anonymous tip that you and the victim were having an affair."

"What? That's nonsense! I didn't even know him!"

"We'll need to take a statement," Harrison said.

I spent the rest of the afternoon telling them the same thing over and over again, while Sassafras wrote it down. After an hour or two of doing that, both cops left, leaving me alone in the room to stare at the walls for over thirty minutes. They returned with my statement, now printed out, for me to sign.

I had never been so upset and frustrated in my entire life.

CHAPTER 17

I was in two minds about the date with Craig. Sure, I had developed a crush on him when I arrived in town, but I had just moved to town after all, and had only recently been through a nasty break up—hardly the best time to think about a new relationship for both reasons.

Thankfully, I hadn't heard from the police since the previous day, so my mood had improved. I was checking my makeup in the bathroom mirror, when there was a knock on the door. I looked at the time on my iPhone. He was five minutes early. Men! I hurried down the hallway and opened the door.

Craig held out another bunch of wildflowers. "I know, flowers last time, but a girl can't have too many flowers, right?"

"They're lovely," I lied, eyeing the wilted flowers. They looked as if they had been picked at the same time as the others the previous day, and had not been put in water. "Thank you. Come in while I put them in a vase."

Craig smiled and stepped in. I showed him into the living room. When I returned with the vase of dead flowers, Craig was hunched over on the sofa.

"Are you okay?" I asked, setting down the vase on the coffee table. Willow appeared and chewed on one of the stems.

"I feel dizzy," Craig said.

"Let's go, then!" I said in an animated fashion. I had not suspected that the house wouldn't like Craig. If his dizziness was due to the house, then I had to get him out of there as soon as possible. I wondered how many other women had to worry about their sentient houses liking their dates. I figured the answer was none.

Craig stood up and clutched at his head. "I don't feel well!" he exclaimed. "My eyes have gone funny. It looks like the walls are closing in on me."

"You need some fresh air." I grabbed his arm and all but dragged him out of the house. When we reached the front gate, I released his arm. "How are you feeling now?"

Craig stood still for a moment and then took a

deep breath. "I feel fine now. That was weird. I hope I'm not coming down with the flu or something. Anyway, let's go. I have reservations."

The short drive to town passed uneventfully. I saw with mixed emotions that we were heading for the Middle Pub. I did like their food, but part of me had hoped that Craig would take me to one of the nice restaurants in the next town. It just seemed as if he wasn't going to any trouble over me.

We walked in the door, and Craig soon found a table with his name on it. Every table was adorned with masses of lilies that overpowered the room with their scent. I picked up the huge vase of lilies in the middle of our table and moved it to the next table. If it had remained, I wouldn't have been able to see Craig sitting across from me. That only left a tealight candle in a small glass bowl and a menu on our table.

"I was scared to ask you out yesterday," Craig said. "I had been wanting to ask you out for a while, but I just chickened out or something each time I was close."

I laughed. "Why?"

"I guess I didn't want to be rejected."

I practically snorted. "Look at you!" I said. "Who would reject you?"

Craig grinned and shrugged his shoulders. "I guess I shouldn't have worried."

"No, you shouldn't have." I saw someone walk past, and looked up automatically. "You've got to be kidding me!"

"What is it?" Craig turned around in his seat. "An ex-boyfriend?"

I laughed. "No." Taking his seat at the small table in the corner, shrouded in shadows, was Alder Vervain.

"He doesn't look like your type," Craig said.

"He's a private detective."

Craig leant forward. "You hired a private detective? You hired him?"

I shook my head. "No. Someone hired him to follow me."

"Who are you? A spy or something?" Craig said in joking tone.

"No," I answered. "It's complicated."

"Oh jeez, you're married, aren't you?"

I laughed. "No, again. Look, you know what happened when I first moved to town, how Brant McCallum died in my shop."

"Right," Craig said. "His fiancée killed him."

I nodded. "And then that realtor died on my porch."

"Yes, that was a coincidence, that's for sure."

I shrugged my shoulders. "Someone hired this guy to follow me around. I guess whoever it is thinks I'm murdering people."

Craig turned around to stare. "That's Alder Vervain isn't it?" he asked.

"You've got good eyesight," I said. "That corner is really dark."

"Well, he's the only private detective I know of," Craig said. "Thinks he's so good, changing his name to make it exotic and all."

I was rather taken aback at Craig's tone. It sounded a little spiteful to me. Perhaps they'd had a run-in at some point. After all, they were around the same age, and had grown up in the same small town. I turned my attention to the menu.

At that point, Craig started into a long story about his sports prowess. I nodded politely, and tried to decide between the zucchini fettuccine, the mushroom crepe, and the Thai red curry. I decided on the Thai red curry and looked up.

Craig was laughing. "Yet I never lost one! They make underage kids wear those masks. I never took a willow in the face. I did break my wrist, but that was playing baseball."

I was embarrassed for the fact that I had no

idea what he hadn't lost, so in an attempt to cover up, I asked, "Did you play every sport?"

He beamed at me. "Nope, just those two. Hey, that's the only time I had to get stitches. It wasn't even playing sport. I wrecked my bike when I was seven, and had to get stitches in my chin."

He seised my finger, prying it from the menu, and stabbed it into his face. I was alarmed until I realised that he, or rather I, was pointing to a shiny white scar just to the left of the dimple in the centre of his chin.

"Oh," I said lamely. I could feel Alder's eyes on me, and that was making me uncomfortable.

Craig got up to order at the counter—there was no table service here—and I squirmed in my seat. I looked around to see if there was a table that would block us from Alder's view. I was so preoccupied that I barely noticed someone sitting in the seat.

"That was fast," I said, looking up, expecting to see Craig. Sadly, it was Kayleen, the mail lady.

"So Miss High and Mighty, you think you're too good to speak to me now?" she snapped at me.

"Sorry?"

"Don't play dumb with me." She leant across the table, her eyes flashing. She was so close that I wondered if the tealight candle would singe her hair. One could only hope.

"Kayleen, I'm sorry if I offended you, but I really don't know what you're talking about," I said in a conciliatory tone.

"The Post Office box!" she screeched. "You got a Post Office box! You did that just to avoid me."

"Oh no," I lied. "It's just easier. It keeps the mail dry when it rains."

"But I always put the mail on your porch when it rains," she said crossly. "Do you think I'm a snoop? Do you think I'm looking through your windows?"

"No," I lied again. I knew that she looked through my windows because she herself had told me that she did. "I thought it would be better to have a Post Office box for your safety too, what with Thomas Hale being found dead on my porch."

Kayleen looked taken aback. "What do you mean?" She removed her hair from the proximity of the candle. I thought I could smell burning hair, but perhaps that was just wishful thinking.

"Well, he was found dead on my porch, and since the mail was pushed under my screen door and it wasn't a rainy day, the police might think you discovered the body before I did. Maybe they even think you killed him."

Kayleen's face grew red. "I did not!" she yelled. "It wasn't a weekday anyway! I don't deliver mail at weekends! Those cops questioned me, and they don't think I did it."

"Did they say that?"

"Well, no." Kayleen fumbled with her handbag. "They would've arrested me if they thought I did it, and they didn't."

"So who do you think killed him?"

A strange look passed across Kayleen's face, but then she composed herself. "I think you did it, Miss Smarty Pants."

Before I could reply, Craig returned to the table. Even in the dim light, I could see he looked distraught to see Kayleen.

Kayleen looked no happier to see Craig. "Are you with her?" she said as she stood up abruptly, knocking the table. She shot me a look of pure poison, and then snatched the bottle of bubbly out of the ice bucket Craig was holding. "French Champagne!" she said angrily, holding it up. "That's a little more expensive than three bucks for a bottle of Passion Pop which I bet you buy for *some* women!"

"Hi, Kayleen," Craig said meekly.

"Hi Kayleen yourself!" She stormed off in a huff, all eyes in the restaurant on her.

"What was that all about?" I asked him.

Craig shrugged, and avoided eye contact. "Who knows? She's crazy."

Call me suspicious, but I was beginning to put two and two together. But really, Craig and Kayleen? That was how it was beginning to look. Still, I counselled myself not to be so distrustful. I had to give him the benefit of the doubt. After all, there could be an innocent explanation.

After Kayleen's outburst, we ate our meal in silence. Craig was unusually subdued. I tried to engage him in conversation, but all my attempts failed. It wasn't a pleasant meal, with Craig's manner and with Alder watching me from the corner. I refused dessert. I just wanted to get home.

"Well, if you don't want dessert, I'd better get you home," Craig said. His mood had changed abruptly, and he was now beaming from ear to ear.

"Thank you for a lovely evening," I said.

Craig winked at me. "The evening's not over yet."

I hoped he didn't mean what I suspected he meant.

CHAPTER 18

Craig stopped his car in front of my house, and jumped out before I could say anything. I joined him at my front gate. "Thanks again," I said, hoping he'd take the hint.

He didn't. Instead, he smiled as he reached to open the little iron gate.

Oh gosh, what to do? "Good night," I said firmly, hoping that would work.

"Huh? Aren't you going to invite me in?" Craig asked, quirking a brow.

I'm never good at thinking on my feet. I typically think up something brilliant to say, but always a good day or so after I need to say it. "Well, remember how you got sick in the house? I spilled some perfume, like a lot, a whole bottle. It doesn't bother me because I'm used to it, I suppose, but it obviously made you sick. I need to air everything out," I finished lamely.

"I don't smell anything, though," he said. "I'm willing to take the risk," he added, winking at me.

Clearly, the fact that I hadn't invited him in was lost on him. "Well, good night then, Craig," I said loudly and firmly. "I will see you some other time. I'm going now. Good night." I slipped past him, and shut the gate between us, exaggerating the movement of shutting the latch. I hurried up the path.

I was fumbling in my handbag for my keys when I heard a noise behind me. I swung around to see Craig coming up the path. Oh dear, he was going to make this difficult.

Craig held up his hands in surrender. "Okay, so you don't want to invite me in," he said. "Okay, I get it. You're a good girl." He smirked at me. "How about just one little kiss?"

I did not like his tone, or his actions, for that matter. "No, Craig," I said. "No. You will have to leave now."

"But that was an expensive bottle of French champagne," he whined. "Surely that deserves one little kiss."

I was horrified. How had I been such a bad

judge of character as to think Craig was dating material? "What do you think I am?" I said in a raised voice.

Craig simply smiled. "I like girls who play hard to get." He stepped closer to me and put his hands on my arms, as his lips approached mine.

Just then, there was a booming sound and Craig flew backwards. He landed on his behind at the bottom of the porch steps.

"How did you do that?" he stammered, his face as white as a sheet.

"I'm an eighth degree black belt in Aikido," I said. "Like Steven Seagal, if you've ever watched one of his old movies." I had no idea why I said that, but it was the first thing that came to mind. "Leave now before I do something worse. Never come back here again—oh, unless there's a fire, of course."

Craig picked himself up, turned and ran.

"Thank you," I said to the house after I watched Craig drive away. "I don't know what I would've done without you."

The encounter had left me shaken up, so I hurried next door to Camino's.

Camino's door slowly opened, making an eerie, creaking sound. "Oh, Amelia. It's you! Is everything okay? You look a bit distressed." Camino ushered me inside. This time, she was wearing a big, brown fleece wombat onesie, complete with giant furry wombat slippers. "Come into the living room, dear. Would you like some tea? We can talk about whatever it is that's bothering you."

"Sure, if you don't mind," I said.

Camino waddled out of the room to fetch the tea, and I crossed to the old fireplace. Above it was an archaic image, an ornately framed oil painting of a regal woman from decades, perhaps centuries, ago. On the mantle below the painting was a medium-sized wooden box that was outlined by a golden frame encrusted with jewels.

Inside the box was a long, wooden object with a pink gem of some sort jutting out from its end.

"Entertained by odd looking things?" Camino asked, marching in with two cups of steaming tea in her hands.

"Oh," I said, turning around. "I was just a bit mesmerised by the box, and then that pink jewel…"

"It's a crystal called rose quartz. It's a beautiful wand. I rarely use it any more."

"Thyme told me that wands are used for casting circles," I said.

Camino nodded. "I used to be a Wiccan

priestess, and so I used it then. It's just not necessary now for the spells I do these days. Still, I keep the wand, as it's an important reminder of my past. Holding onto the past is crucial," she continued. "Take that painting over the fireplace, for instance. I wouldn't say it's the most beautiful thing I've ever seen, but she is one of my ancestors. If you look around, you'll see the influence of years past everywhere. It's difficult to understand the future without knowing about your history, so I like to collect what you might consider oddities."

I smiled. "That's part of the reason why I always run to your door when I'm in a jam," I said, earning a chuckle from Camino. "You seem to know a lot more about this stuff than most people."

"Well, that comes with being old, I guess," Camino said with a laugh, "not that I feel old. Now, what is it you needed me for this time?" She handed me one of the cups of tea. "Please have a seat and tell me your troubles."

I sat on the sofa. "Thank you," I said. "It's about my house again."

"What happened this time?" she asked. "Is it closing its walls on another poor soul?"

"Yes, but not just anyone this time."

Camino's brow furrowed. "Tell me what happened."

"It's Craig. When he came over to pick me up for our date, he said he wasn't feeling well and kept making comments about the walls closing in around him. I got him out of there as fast as I could."

"Hmm, well that is a bit peculiar," Camino replied. "There must be something about Craig that the house dislikes, but what could it be? He's always seemed like a nice, pleasant man to me." She leant forward in her seat and scratched her chin, looking up towards the ceiling as if it would offer her some sound advice. "Are you sure that he's as nice as you think he is?"

I shook my head. "That's just it," I said. "No, he's not. I found that out tonight. I suspect he's involved with Kayleen the post lady, and after dinner, he wanted me to invite him inside. I didn't, but after I tried to get rid of him, he followed me to the front door and tried to kiss me. The house threw him into the yard."

Camino stood up and walked over to the fire-place. She looked back at me and sighed. "Good-ness me," she said. "What a state of affairs. The house always knows. The house always sees things that we miss. Well, you have had a lucky escape, my dear. I just hope you're not too upset about discovering the man's true character."

I thought for a moment. "No," I said honestly. "I was attracted to him when I first moved to town, but it was just a bit of a crush. The problem now is, what if he's the killer?"

Camino looked taken aback, so I pressed on. "As everyone in town knows, Kayleen works part time cleaning at the hospital, so I figured she might be able to steal insulin. What if she has an accomplice, Craig?"

"But what possible motive would Kayleen have for doing away with that poor man?"

"Is there a spell or something that we can cast to find out why the house dislikes someone?" I asked.

Camino shook her head. "No, not as such. Yet sometimes figuring that out is not simply a matter of casting spells. We have to do our own part. For example, there is no use doing a spell to get a job if one doesn't answer job applications. The two must go hand in hand. We just have to look at things with an investigative eye."

"Okay, but how do we do that?"

"Easy," Camino said. "We need to know more about Craig."

I shook my head. "I'm not sure what you mean."

"Until today, you saw Craig in a different light from what your house does. Tell me what you saw," she said.

"Well, whenever he was around me, he was usually polite, even sweet. He was never rude or unpleasant in any way." I rubbed my forehead. "That's why I was so thrown off by the interaction between him and Kayleen, and the way he acted when he took me home. I can't possibly see how he'd be the one framing me. I'd believe it of Kayleen, but not of him. I just wish I could communicate with my house and understand what it's doing and why."

"It's doing what it is to protect you, as I've said time and time again," Camino said. "We might not understand how or why, but that's what it is trying to do. The house might not think he's the murderer. It could be something such as cheating on girl-friends, or it could be something much worse. It's impossible to know until we figure out what the house is focusing on. There must be some negative energy coming from Craig, but there's just no way to determine what's sending those vibes to the house."

I nodded. I turned my back to the window and glanced around the room. The wand still sat in its wooden box over the fireplace as Camino's ancestor watched over it. On the far wall was a bookcase of old tomes with titles in Latin and various other lost languages embossed on them with a gold flourish. A shelf opposite the bookcase held various bottles of potions and elixirs.

Camino walked over to the sofa and sat next to me. "We need to be grateful to the house. For all we know, he is a no good cheater or a liar, and you deserve much better than that."

I nodded, looking out the window. I wondered where Craig was at that very moment. Was he with another, unsuspecting woman? Was that why my house didn't like him? Or was it because he was a murderer?

CHAPTER 19

I was on my way to Ruprecht's shop with Thyme. It was just turning to dusk. The streets were aglow with artificial orange light reflecting from the rain-drenched streets. Camino had been the one to propose the meeting. She had come up with the idea to perform a spell designed to reveal my enemies.

Once again, I found myself at the forefront of a dangerous game, one that I wasn't sure I wanted to play. The only thing that made me feel safe was my group of friends. It was amazing to me to think that few months ago I had been a normal young woman, fresh out of a relationship, unsure where life was going to take me. Since inheriting my aunt's house and moving to Bayberry Creek, everything had changed. I was no longer content to see where life took me—now, I was the one taking charge. And despite the fact I didn't always make the right choices, I was happy that I had choices to make.

Ruprecht's shop was dark when we parked in front of it, although I could make out a dim light burning. Ruprecht himself answered the door, pulling it open a moment before Thyme could knock.

"Hello, my dears," he said with a smile. "Do come in. You're the last to arrive."

"This one is always running late," Thyme said, hitching her thumb at me.

I shrugged. "It's either a character flaw, or a charming quirk."

"I think it's quite charming," Ruprecht said over his shoulder. "Except when I'm the one waiting for you."

I laughed and apologised. We followed him to the back of the shop. Camino and Mint were already sitting at the table. Ruprecht took a seat at the head of the table.

"Friends," Ruprecht said with a soft smile. "I'm glad you could all make it, at the behest of our dear Camino. I think perhaps we should get to work before any discussion, because that in itself will set our discussion on the right path."

The others nodded their agreement, and Camino stood. She picked up a bag from the floor beside her chair and pulled a few items from it. The first was a thick candle made of yellow and purple wax. It had a long white wick that had yet to be burned. After she placed the candle on a fireproof dish, she reached into her bag and pulled out a small vial of yellow liquid. She set that on its side next to the candle and continued extracting items from her bag: a piece of thin parchment paper, and a grease pencil. Camino sat down once more, and then took up the grease pencil as she smoothed the parchment out before her with one hand. She began to write.

I watched with interest. I craned my neck to see what Camino was writing, but I couldn't quite make it out.

Thyme produced a book of matches and prized one free from the others, closing the flimsy cardboard lid over the end of it, and striking it along the scratchy strip. It lit at once, a small yellow and orange flame that danced in the dim light of the store. Thyme reached across the table and lit the candle. When the wick caught, it produced a much larger flame than the match, and began to crackle and sputter, almost like a firecracker. The flame died down and danced slowly along the wick, twisting this way and that as it rose into the air, the flame turning into a spiralling grey stream of smoke.

When Camino was finished writing, she pushed the paper towards me and set her fingers on one corner, turning it so I could see what had been transcribed. It simply read, in slanting scrawl, 'Who works against Amelia's highest good?'

There were symbols drawn around the edges of the parchment, figures I didn't recognise, but the words were in English. I was touched that once again a spell was being done for my benefit.

Camino pulled the thin and waxy parchment back towards her and then set the burning candle on it. She took up the vial next, pulling out the small rubber stopper with an audible pop. She held her index finger over the opening and twisted her wrist so that the oil inside coated the tip of her finger. She wiped her finger up the surface of the candle in several strokes.

"Show us who works against Amelia's highest good," Camino said, her voice soft and low. "Reveal to us who poses her harm, and who does not have her best interests at heart. Do this. Do this."

Thyme turned to me. "Let's leave the room now," she said in a whisper. "Camino is going to do a divination as soon as she feels the time is right. We need to leave her alone."

I rose and followed the others out of the room into the tiny kitchen. "How long does it take?" I asked in hushed tones.

"As long as it takes," Mint said with a shrug. "These things aren't always exact. It doesn't usually take too long, though."

"It should help us find who is behind all of this," Thyme said. "It mightn't tell us who Thomas Hale's killer is, but it will tell us if Alder Vervain is someone we need to worry about."

I was somewhat irritated. Thyme was already convinced that Alder was not to be trusted. It seemed to me that she was firmly convinced of that, and didn't need a spell to reveal his true intentions.

And then there was Craig. Sure, he wasn't the knight in shining armour that I'd first thought, but that didn't mean he was a killer, and someone trying to frame me for the murder. I felt light headed all of a sudden. "I've got a headache coming on. Do you mind if I go outside for some fresh air?"

Ruprecht looked at me with concern. "Are you all right? Would you like some lavender tea?"

I shook my head. "I'm okay, thanks. I just need

some fresh air for a few moments. I'll be right back."

I headed for the front door. I turned the lock and pushed the door open, escaping into the cool air on the footpath. I closed my eyes and took a deep breath. Sometimes all this stuff was just too much. The living house, me being a witch, the two murders on my property, the almost-boyfriend who was not to be trusted.

"Are you okay?" a deep voice said beside me.

I jumped. It was Alder Vervain.

"What do you want?" My words came out more harshly than I intended.

"Well, I'm following you, as you know. I was worried about you. You look tired."

"I am tired," I said. "I'm mostly tired of you following me."

Alder chuckled. "I'm sure you are," he said, "but I have bills to pay. Apart from that, I just wanted to check up on you."

"Why?"

"People aren't always who you think they are. Now, about that guy you're seeing…"

I held up my hand to cut him off. "I'm not seeing him."

Alder nodded, and I wondered if he already knew. "What are you doing at *Glinda's?*"

"That's none of your business," I said, remembering that Alder's family had a history of persecuting witches.

"Fair enough," he said, "but watch your back. People aren't always what they seem." He stepped backwards, into the shadows, and soon merged with the falling darkness.

I watched him go, and then went back inside.

"That was good timing," Thyme said. "I was just about to come and get you. Camino's ready."

The others were already at the table, and I took my seat. Camino held a pendulum, a cylindrical clear crystal quartz pointed at one end and hanging from a delicate gold chain.

In front of her were several pieces of paper, scrunched up into balls and arranged in a circle. Mint leant over to me. "There are names written inside the papers," she said. "The names are hidden while Camino does the divination, so she won't be subconsciously influenced by them."

I nodded. "What names are in there?"

"Alder Vervain, Craig, Kayleen, Dianne, and Unknown," she whispered. "We always do a paper labelled 'Unknown' in case it's someone we haven't thought of."

That makes sense, I thought, as I turned my attention to the pendulum. I didn't know why Dianne's name was included, but I supposed it was a good idea to include her, as she had known the deceased.

At first the pendulum did nothing, and I wondered if anything at all would happen. Then, as Camino chanted softly, it began to move. It moved violently over one piece of paper again and again. Camino stilled the pendulum, and then moved the paper from the circle, placing it to one side.

As she chanted again, the pendulum swung between two pieces of paper. It was nowhere near as forceful this time, but moved rhythmically. Camino once more stilled the pendulum, and moved those two pieces of paper from the circle, placing them side-by-side under the first piece of paper.

Camino returned to her chanting, but this time, the pendulum did nothing. After a few moments, she opened her eyes. White smoke rose lazily from the hot wick as she snuffed the candle.

Everyone looked at me with concern. I was worried, too. Three people did not have my best interests at heart? That sounded bad, real bad. Part of me wanted to know who they were, but part of me didn't.

I jumped when the room suddenly flooded with light. I looked up and saw Ruprecht at the light switch. He at once returned to his seat, just as Camino opened one of the two pieces of paper at the bottom of the arrangement. Those were the two pieces of paper that had not drawn any reaction from the pendulum. She flattened out the paper and then held it up for all of us to see. It had the word, 'Unknown.'

Okay, that was a concern. I'd rather someone unknown have ill intent towards me, because that meant that three people I knew had it in for me, at least to some degree.

Camino then reached for the top piece of paper, the piece to which the pendulum had reacted violently. She unfolded it, and then flattened it. Everyone gasped when she held it up to show us the name.

Dianne.

Still, no one spoke. I wanted to ask questions, wanted to ask why Dianne would mean me harm. Yet the others were silent, so I remained silent also. There were three more pieces of paper to go, including two more names of people who did not have my best interests at heart. Camino reached for one of those. I held my breath as she held it up.

Kayleen.

Well, that was no surprise. Kayleen had been clearly upset to see Craig having dinner with me, and I suspected that they had something going on. At any rate, she was angry that I had a Post Office box. Or was there more to it?

I turned my attention to the last two pieces of paper. Only the names of Craig and Alder remained. Which one did not have my best interests at heart?

Camino reached for the paper that had been next to Kayleen's. She carefully, and it seemed to me, way too slowly, unscrunched it, and then placed it face down on the table, flattening it out. She held it up to reveal the name.

Everyone gasped.

CHAPTER 20

"Something went wrong," Mint said, shaking her head. "Right?"

"I don't think so," Ruprecht said. "It didn't seem wrong."

Mint wouldn't give up. "But Dianne is the woman Amelia is trying to help. Why would she be out to harm her?"

"And why did Alder Vervain come up innocent?" Thyme asked, reaching for the remaining piece of paper, the one that, like 'Unknown,' meant me no harm. Sure enough, it had the words 'Alder Vervain' written on it. I breathed a sigh of relief.

"It is what it is," Ruprecht said. "We need to take it at face value."

My relief was short lived when the full import

of what had just happened sank in. "Does this mean that three people are out to harm me?"

Camino rushed to reassure me. "No, not at all. It just means they don't have your best interests at heart. As far as Kayleen goes, well, the woman has a grudge against just about everyone in town. As for Craig, it could just mean he's a womaniser. Yes, it could be more than that, but it might not be. The one who really stood out was Dianne. "

"What would Dianne have against me?" I asked.

No one seemed to have an answer for that.

"We need to do some digging on Dianne," Thyme said finally. "I think."

Ruprecht nodded. "She's right. We were here thinking Dianne was the reason we were doing this. You and Amelia were trying to help her, but it seems that she has an agenda of her own. And as for Craig," he continued, "it would be best to stay away from him. Certainly he shouldn't be going inside your home."

"Don't worry. I'll be avoiding him like the plague from now on."

Ruprecht nodded and patted my arm.

"Why don't I invite Dianne over for coffee and

cake?" I suggested. "The house will probably do something to reveal what she's up to."

"That's a good idea," Thyme said. "I should be there, too. We'll make it a girls' cupcake evening."

And so, the following afternoon, I was waiting nervously for Dianne to show up at my house. I felt betrayed. I had been nothing but nice to the woman, so I had not the faintest clue why she would have a problem with me.

I greeted Dianne at the door with false enthusiasm.

If Dianne felt anything at all from the house, she did a good job of keeping it to herself. "Girl chat with coffee sounded exactly like what Madam Dianne needed," she said. "Thanks for having me."

"Any time," I said, as I shut the door behind her. As I showed Dianne into the living room, Thyme came in with a tray loaded with coffee cups and a carafe of coffee.

"Here we are," Thyme said, setting the tray down beside a large box of cupcakes.

"Let me use the bathroom, if I may," Dianne said.

As soon as she was out of sight, Thyme hurried over to me. "She might not make it back," she whispered.

I shook my head. "She seemed fine. I don't understand it. I thought she'd be dizzy by now."

Thyme shrugged. "She might be good at hiding it."

I nudged her. "Shush! I think she's coming back."

Dianne returned and looked completely normal, much to my puzzlement. I offered her a plate of double chocolate cupcakes.

Dianne waved her hand in refusal.

"But they're your favourite," I said.

She shook her head. "No, I can't. My doctor is nagging me," she said. "I've been having dizzy spells and my blood tests came back bad. I have to take my diabetes more seriously."

I exchanged glances with Thyme. "I didn't know you had diabetes," Thyme said.

Dianne looked as if she had said something she shouldn't have. She fidgeted with her coffee cup and then set it down. "It's just something I have to deal with. I don't talk about it much."

"Well, I'm sorry to hear you suffer from it," Thyme said. "It can certainly be a terrible disease."

"It becomes second nature after a while," Dianne said. "But it keeps me from those cupcakes sometimes."

I faked a laugh. All I could think of was the insulin. Thomas Hale had been killed with insulin. Yet what could be her motive? She said she had barely known the man, but if she killed him, of course she'd say that.

When Dianne next used the bathroom, Thyme hurried over to me. "Insulin!" she said.

"I know, right!"

Thyme nodded. "I bet she was the one who killed Hale with insulin."

"So now we've gone from wanting to help her to thinking she's a murderer?" I asked.

Thyme pulled a face. "I don't know, but she showed up on the paper, didn't she!"

I agreed. "She sure did."

"And did you see her face, when she realised she told us she was diabetic? Why wouldn't she want anyone to know?" Thyme asked.

"She might be private," I said. "Okay, I don't believe that. Something's up with the diabetic thing, but we're forgetting something."

"What?"

"She was at the top of the list, but she's been in my house for over an hour now."

Thyme nodded. "And nothing's happened."

"Not a thing. The cats are hiding from her,

though." As if on cue, Willow and Hawthorn peeped around the corner.

An idea occurred to me. "What if the house wanted us to know about the diabetes? Maybe the house knew what we were doing. It didn't need to warn us."

"Possibly. So what's the next step?" Thyme asked.

"We need to find out if she has a motive. Did she know Hale after all? Is there a history there, something more than a passing acquaintance?"

"How are we going to do that?" Thyme asked.

"We can figure it out when she goes, if you have time to hang around for a while."

"Sure," Thyme said, "but I've thought of something else. Craig is also a suspect. We have to consider the fact that the house didn't react to Dianne, but did react to Craig."

"This is doing my head in," I said.

Thyme grabbed my arm. "We're talking about Dianne as if she's guilty of murder, but she didn't get dizzy or think the walls were closing in on her. Yet when Craig came over, as soon as he stepped onto your porch, he got dizzy. The house attacked him twice."

"What are you saying?" I asked urgently, as I heard the bathroom door shut. "I thought the house only attacked him as he's a womaniser."

"Maybe, maybe not," Thyme said, "but what if Craig is the murderer?"

CHAPTER 21

I was driving around Newcastle, and I was lost. "I don't know if this is such a good idea, Thyme," I said for the umpteenth time, as yet another impatient driver blasted their horn at me.

"Pull over and I'll google the directions again," she said. "The connection just dropped out."

I sighed and gripped the steering wheel. "Thyme, if you look out the window, you will see that I can't pull over, unless you want me to drive over the cliff into the sea." We were driving up a long, winding hill from Nobbys Beach in search of the café where Dianne used to work. There was a white rail beside us, and then, a fair distance below, was the sea. Huge waves crashed against Newcastle Beach.

"There!" she screeched. "King Edward Park. Do you see the sign? Pull over there."

I swung the wheel hard and ended up on a narrow road. I parked next to a 'No Parking' sign. "I'll keep the engine running and watch out for cops while you google the directions," I said. "I don't know why you didn't bring your scrying water."

Thyme looked up. "Are you kidding? There'd be no water left in it by the time we got here, the way you drive."

I pouted. I still hadn't told Thyme that I had seen images in the scrying water. I wasn't exactly keeping it from her, but I was still coming to terms with the fact that I was a witch.

"There it is," Thyme said triumphantly, followed not so triumphantly by, "Oh, I think we just passed it. The turn off, at any rate. Now you need to go down Watt Street."

I sighed loudly and turned the car around. It had taken four hours to get here. I wondered if there was any point to the entire trip.

"Quick, turn left!"

I did as Thyme said, and found myself in Hunter Street. A few minutes later, after driving once again beside the sea, Thyme directed me to pull over outside a large brick building. "I thought she worked in a café?" I asked. "So why does that sign say 'Antique Centre?'"

Thyme shook her head. "It says it's here on the map."

"What do we do now?"

"Drive around a little. If we see someone, we can ask them."

I edged the car forward, but I had only gone a few yards when I saw a sign partially obscured behind a half-dead shrub. "Thyme, look!"

"Waterside Eatery," Thyme said aloud. "Yay, we found it!"

I turned left into a parking area, although there was only one vacant spot, and it was hard to manoeuvre despite the fact it was a small car. The parking was free, the only free parking I had seen since we'd arrived in Newcastle.

I got out of the car and looked around. "Waterside Eatery?" I said. "Roadside, more like it. The water is over there." I pointed to the harbour.

"At least you can see the water between the buildings," Thyme said.

I shrugged. I was nervous now that we were here. On the one hand, we could have wasted a day, and Ruprecht and Camino would have wasted a day minding the shop for me. On the other hand, there was a chance we would find out if Dianne knew Thomas Hale more than as a realtor-client relationship. If so, that would give us something to take to the police.

I opened the big glass door for Thyme to go inside. "Let's go and see if any of her old co-workers want to talk."

The interior was bright and trendy. Carefully mismatched chairs sat at carefully mismatched tables. The furniture was up-cycled and chalk-painted. Equally trendy patrons lounged around, drinking green smoothies and reading newspapers.

I walked right up to the counter. "Hi, we're looking for a friend of ours, Dianne Longley. She used to work here, but we've lost touch with her."

The waitress paused for a few moments. "Wait, the lady with all the blue eye makeup?"

I glanced over at Thyme to see her hand over her mouth. She was doing her best not to laugh.

I nodded. "Yes, that's Dianne. You wouldn't happen to know any of her friends around here, would you? Or where she might be hanging out?"

"I didn't know her that well. I only work part time, and we never did the same shifts. Every Friday night I'd relieve her, though. She always went out to that bar across the road with her friends."

"Is anyone else working here today that knew her?"

The waitress shook her head. "Sorry."

As we turned to leave, she called us back. "One of the girls who used to work here works over at the bar now. She was a good friend of Dianne's."

We thanked her and walked back outside. "You don't want to go in there, do you?" Thyme asked.

"It's not that I don't want to go in," I said. "I'm just not sure what to expect when we do."

"Just remember our plan. I'm getting married and want to invite her to my wedding. If we find anyone that knows her, we'll find out if they knew Thomas Hale, too."

I nodded. "Okay, let's do this."

The bar was dark inside, and there were hardly any people in sight. I figured it only came alive at night.

"What can I get you?" the bored bartender asked. He didn't look up from polishing a glass.

"We're actually here looking for a friend," I said. "Would you happen to know a woman named Dianne Longley who used to come here a lot?"

"I just started a few days ago," he said with a

shrug. "You could ask Charlie over there, though." He pointed towards an old man who sat by himself at the edge of the bar. "He's a regular here."

"Thank you."

As we approached the man, I was hit by the strong smell of whiskey. I hoped the man was coherent, and that his memory wasn't fried by alcohol. "Hello, ladies, lovely day for a drink," he murmured, fumbling with his glass.

"We're looking for a friend," Thyme said. "Have you ever met a woman by the name of Dianne Longley? She used to come here every Friday night."

After the man chugged at his drink, he slammed the glass down on the counter and smiled at us. "Tom Hale's girl? She hasn't been in here lately. Neither has he, come to think of it," he said with a loud burp.

Thyme and I gasped and looked at each other.

"What do you mean, she was his girl?" I asked him.

"Those two lovebirds! They used to come in here all the time together, always draped all over each other. They were supposed to be moving away together, but that was the last I heard from either of them." He polished off the rest of his drink in one gulp.

"Excuse me, is there something I can help you two with?" a woman's voice said from behind us. "Why are you asking so many questions about Dianne?"

"We're old friends of hers," Thyme said. "I'm getting married and I wanted to invite her to the wedding."

The woman crossed her arms over her chest and jutted out her chin. "Are you cops? They've been in here asking questions."

"No, of course not," I said. "We're old friends of hers."

The woman clearly did not believe us. "What are your names?" she snapped. "I'll make sure Dianne gets in touch with you."

"Um, we're the Winchester sisters," I said. "I'm Samantha and this is Deanna. Dianne has our numbers. Tell her to call us, will you?"

With that, we beat a hasty retreat. We didn't speak again until we were in the car, and driving out of the parking lot.

Finally, Thyme spoke. "Are you nuts? Samantha and Deanna Winchester? What if Dianne's friend is a *Supernatural* fan?"

I chuckled. "Well, it was the first thing I thought of, and you didn't come up with anything better. Besides, Dianne will know it was us as soon as her friend describes us. At least we got what we came here for. We now know that Dianne and Thomas Hale were good friends—and more than just friends, by the sound of it."

Thyme shook her head. "That man was hardly the most reliable witness."

"Still, he knew Thomas Hale, didn't he?"

"I don't understand why the police didn't figure this out," Thyme said.

I shrugged, and slammed on the brakes when a bicycle pulled out in front of me. "No idea. Perhaps that old man wasn't here when they went in to question people, and her friend wouldn't tell them anything. Besides, Dianne did admit to being his client. That would throw them off the track."

"So we're thinking Dianne's the murderer now?"

I nodded. "Sadly, yes. It sure looks that way."

CHAPTER 22

"*A*re we there yet?" Thyme asked, sitting up and rubbing her eyes.

"Almost," I said. "Did all that excitement back there tire you out?"

Thyme shook her head. "I'm just worried what Dianne will do when her friend tells her we were snooping around."

"That's why we're going straight to the police station."

Thyme peered out her window. "Like I keep saying, I don't think they're open this late."

"And like I keep saying," I said, "we can just drive past and see if their lights are on. If they're shut, we'll just go back in the morning. With any luck, they might've already arrested her, since you left a message for the detectives that she's diabetic. They didn't call you back about that, did they?"

Thyme shook her head. "No, but the desk sergeant said he'd pass it on."

"I just hope they don't get mad that we went snooping around for information."

"We don't have a choice," Thyme said. "It's too late to turn back now."

Surprisingly, there was a light shining from the windows of the Bayberry Creek police station.

I climbed out of the car and stretched. My back was sore from sitting in the car for so long.

I blinked hard when the door opened into a brightly lit foyer. I pressed the buzzer. It chimed, echoing around the empty room. After a few moments, a heavyset man in a blue uniform appeared. "What can I do for you?"

"Is Detective Harrison in?" I asked him. "Or Detective Sassafras?"

"What do you want to speak them about?" the cop asked.

I bit my lip. He wasn't going to make this easy. "We have some information for them about Thomas Hale's murder," I said. "I'm Amelia Spelled. I was the one who discovered his body on my porch. The detectives were sent photos of me with the victim and they discovered they were faked. They asked me if I knew who would want to frame me."

The sergeant just looked at me. "Go on," he said after an interval.

"Well, now I do know who framed me," I said. "Dianne Longley. She told the detectives that Thomas Hale was only her realtor, but they were dating."

"And you know this because?" he said gruffly.

Thyme and I exchanged glances. I took a deep breath. "Well, today we went to Newcastle to where Dianne used to work, and we were told that Dianne and Thomas Hale were always draped all over each other like lovebirds."

The cop held up his hand and his face turned beet red. "Wait! You two went all the way to Newcastle by yourselves to ask questions about a murder suspect? Do you have any idea how dangerous that is?" he barked. "I could arrest you both right now for that. What do you think you are, amateur sleuths or something? This isn't a game!"

"Of course it's not a game," Thyme said, "but you guys have had my friend in your sights since that poor man's body was found. You've had her in for questioning twice. Now we have information to give you."

I held my breath waiting for the cop's response. "And the information is?"

"Like I said, Dianne and Thomas weren't just passing acquaintances—they were in a relationship," I said.

"Who told you that?"

"It was one of her friends from the bar that she and Thomas frequented every Friday night before moving here," I said. "The bar is right across from where she worked, the Waterside Eatery."

"All right. I'll pass that information onto the detectives."

Thyme leant forward. "Do they already have the information that Dianne is a diabetic?"

"Detective Harrison and Defective Sassafras are in Sydney for a court hearing," the cop said. "This information will be passed along to them. Now you two are to stay away from this investigation. There will be no more sticking your noses into this case. Let us handle it."

"But..." Thyme began.

"I'll let you ladies in on a secret," the cop said. "We're the police, and this is an ongoing investigation. To be quite honest, and this might shock you, we're already looking into it. We're looking into it, because that's our job. Now, it's not your job to go running around digging stuff up. You don't have a badge, do you?"

When neither of us said anything, the cop asked again. "Do either of you have a badge?"

"No," we said in unison.

"Then I suggest you leave this for us, and head on home."

We left at that point—there was no use saying anything else. I was upset, but Thyme seemed to be in better spirits. "He really had to say that to us," she said when we were back in my car. "The main thing is that the detectives will get the information."

"I hope they get it in a hurry," I said. "It's bad timing that they're in Sydney right now."

Thyme shook her head. "Don't worry. They can tell the local cops what to do. They can order them to arrest Dianne."

"I suppose so. Anyway, why did Dianne try to frame me? I still don't understand it."

"Possibly because Thomas Hale was found on your porch, so you were the easiest scapegoat, I suppose, but who knows? I dare say you'll find out, eventually."

I dropped off Thyme before heading home. I

refused her offer of dinner. I was tired and wanted a long bath, a glass of wine, and to watch something mindless and comforting on TV—if the house would let me.

I stepped inside, happy to be home. It had been a long day. The living room was bathed in shadow, and the cats were nowhere to be seen. I dropped my handbag and keys onto the coffee table and then yawned and stretched.

When the knock came on the door, my first thought was that it was the police. Had I not been so tired, I likely would not have answered the door. Anyway, I did, and there was Dianne standing on my doorstep.

She had something in her hand, and for one wild moment I was sure it was a gun. The woman stepped forward and blue arcs of energy crackled at the end of the Taser I had mistaken for a firearm.

"Let's have a little talk," she said.

CHAPTER 23

I knew I didn't have a choice. If Dianne wanted to talk, that's just what we were going to do. It was hard to argue with a crazy person who had a Taser held close to my face.

"I know you've figured it out," Dianne said.

I looked at her. The portly woman was dishevelled, her face red and sweaty, her clothes wrinkly. "A friend of mine from Newcastle called me and said that two women were asking questions about me. I know it was you and Thyme."

"What are you talking about?" I said, doing my best to sound genuinely puzzled. "Please put that thing down."

Dianne laughed. She pressed the flat red button on the side of her Taser again, and blue electricity arced between the two raised metal prongs at the end of the device. "You forget that Madam Dianne is psychic. I had a vision of Thyme driving you there in her car. You can't lie to me. No more lies."

I took a step backwards. Clearly, she wasn't psychic, and she had just gotten it wrong again. Nevertheless, now was not the time and place to point that out to her.

I summed up the situation. Dianne was a crazy woman who had killed a man, and probably intended to kill me, too. In fact, Dianne could come at me at any moment. On the other hand, while I didn't know much about Tasers, I didn't think that they were fatal. Well, I hoped not, anyway. Then there was the fact that I was much fitter than Dianne, so I should be able to overpower her in a struggle. And then there was my house. It wasn't attacking her yet, no doubt for reasons of its own, but I was certain that it would, when crunch came to crunch. All in all, the situation probably wasn't as bad as it looked, but that didn't stop my heart beating out of my chest and my palms sweating.

We stood just inside the door, which Dianne had swung shut with her hip. "You two fancy yourselves as wannabe cops, solving a crime," she snapped at me. "Go sit on the couch."

I nodded and backed away slowly. There was no

way I was going to turn my back on her. When I felt the back of my legs bump into my coffee table, I skirted around it and then sat on my couch. Dianne came forward, but remained standing.

"So you went snooping around and asking questions about me," she said. "And you found out what exactly?"

"I found out you and Hale had a thing," I said.

That was apparently the wrong thing to say, as Dianne exploded, her face contorting into a mask of rage. "A thing? A thing? It was a lot more than a thing! We were in love!"

"Okay, I'm sorry!" I said quickly. "I found out you two were in love."

"And your friend knows this, too?"

"Thyme? Yes, she knows."

"All right then, I guess I'll have to pay her a visit when I'm done here."

My stomach knotted. That certainly sounded as though Dianne did indeed plan on killing me, and then Thyme.

"He was divorcing his wife," Dianne said suddenly, the rage building on her features. "Well, so he said when we started dating. He told me he was married; he never hid it from me. Some men might have, but Tom was a good man. He had a good job. He was divorcing his wife. They didn't have kids, but you know how divorce can be. He was sure his wife would get his money, everything he'd worked so hard for. That's why he was taking it slowly."

I wondered why she had killed him. Her story certainly didn't sound as if it was leading up to murder.

Dianne was still talking. "We moved here together, but were living apart until he got his divorce. I had been driving around looking to buy a Victorian house with a nice garden, and I saw this house. I knew it wasn't for sale, but Tom suggested we go and see if the owner would be interested in selling. I didn't know you lived here at the time." She looked at me.

I nodded.

"Tom had been acting strange since we arrived in town," she said. "I was living in a rental and he was staying in a motel. Tom had been quiet all that day. We were on your porch, and I knew something was wrong. I challenged him—I told him to tell me what was wrong. He finally said that he was sorry, but he had decided to try to make it work with his wife. He told me he loved me, but he said he loved her, too. Are you listening?"

"Yes," I said firmly. "Please go on."

She shot me a strange look. "I wasn't thinking. I didn't mean to do it. I just got very upset all of a sudden. I reached into my handbag and grabbed my insulin and I just jabbed him with it. Right in the neck. I slammed the plunger down. Then I realised what I'd done and I was shocked. I didn't realise I had done it. It all happened in slow motion. I don't really feel like it was me doing it. I remember it all, but it's like a movie or something. It still doesn't feel like real life. It's all surreal."

"Why don't you tell the police that?" I said in a placating tone. "I'm sure they'd go easy on you, given the circumstances."

"Do you take me for an idiot?" she yelled. "Murder is murder! It's not like it was self defence or anything!"

"Why did you Photoshop those photos of me and send them to the police? And put photos of me in his wallet?"

Dianne's eyes opened wide, but she did calm down somewhat. "That's obvious. I was their only suspect, so I had to find them another one. As he died on your porch, you were the obvious person."

"And how did you keep the fact that you were diabetic from them?"

Dianne shot me a look. "That was easy. I simply denied that I was. They searched my house, but I knew that they would, so I took all my insulin, syringes, and my blood glucose meter to the park and hid them under a bottle brush bush."

"So what are you going to do with me?"

Dianne sighed. "You're the only one who knows. Well, you and Thyme. So I'll have to make sure neither of you can ever tell anyone."

"But we've already told the police," I said. "I've just come from the police station. They know you and Thomas Hale were in a relationship, and they know you're diabetic. You have the murder weapon, and you have the motive."

"You interfering fool," Diane screamed, lunging at me with the Taser. "They didn't find out anything much by themselves. They wouldn't have figured it out if you hadn't told them!"

As she lunged at me, Willow appeared from nowhere and ran between her legs. Dianne collapsed in a heap on the floor, the Taser flying from her hands into the fire grate.

I ran for the Taser, but Dianne caught my leg as I went past, and held onto it. I struggled not to fall. I twisted and turned, pulling myself from Dianne's grasp and teetering forward. "Help me!" I yelled at the house.

"You're crazy," Dianne said. "Why would I help you?" She grabbed a handful of my hair and yanked it hard.

I fell backwards, right on top of Dianne. She wrapped her arms around me and flipped us both over. I could barely move, let alone breathe, with the heavier woman on top of me. I was relieved that she hadn't managed to retrieve the Taser.

I pinched Dianne's neck hard. She yelled and rolled over. I wriggled out from under her and tried to stand up, but she again grabbed my leg and held it hard in a vice-like grip.

There was a vase on the mantelpiece, or to be precise, a blue and white ginger jar, most likely an antique, which had belonged to my aunt. I reached up over my head, and could just wrap my fingers around it. I pulled, but nothing happened. That was weird. I knew it wasn't glued there; I'd removed it to dust it only the other day.

Dianne pulled herself to her feet, using me to support herself. If only I could get the vase free and smash it over her head, yet it wouldn't budge. After a moment or two, it dawned on me that the house didn't want me to break the vase. "Let go!" I yelled at the house. "Let go!"

"I won't let go!" Dianne said. She shoved me backwards and then bit my leg.

"Ouch!" I screamed, and pulled her hair hard. It came right off in my hands. I screamed again. Thankfully, it was a wig.

In one motion, I threw the wig in Dianne's face and threw myself at the coffee table. By some miracle, it still had the vase of dead wildflowers Craig had given me on it. I landed too hard on the coffee table, which then broke apart. The vase fell and shattered, spraying me with water and dead wildflowers.

I picked up the top of the coffee table and shoved it forward. It slammed into Dianne's shins, and she shrieked and fell sideways, throwing her hands in the air.

It was then that the house laughed. It sounded like thunder, but was a deep belly laugh, rolling and rumbling with mirth. It was followed by a clapping sound.

"You're enjoying this, aren't you?" I yelled at the house. "This is not a Mixed Martial Arts tournament! This is real life! I could get hurt!"

"That's what I'm counting on," Dianne said.

I looked up to see that she had scrambled to her feet, and was pulling a syringe from her handbag. Her eyes glittered. "Insulin," she said menacingly.

I summed up the situation. She was between the front door and me. I looked at the Taser lying in the fireplace. Before I could decide whether to try to reach it, there was a loud banging on the front door.

"Police! Open up!"

"No!" Dianne yelled. "Go away! Get back in your car, or I'll kill this woman!"

"Who is that?" the voice called.

I saw another cop at the front window, peering in. He turned away. "The suspect has a hostage!" he shouted.

"I want you to leave!" Dianne yelled at the window. "I won't go down for this! I didn't do anything—Amelia did it. She's framing me!"

"Step away from Ms Spelled," the cop at the window said calmly.

"I want out of this!" Dianne screamed. "Go away or she gets it!"

The cop vanished from sight.

"Get away from the Taser," Dianne said to me. "Go over there, into the corner."

I did as she asked.

Dianne, keeping her eyes on me, stepped over to the fireplace and then reached in for the Taser. As she did, her arm passed through the grate. "What the?" she screamed.

Dianne kept disappearing, until just her head was showing above the grate.

I was shocked beyond measure. I knew the house could make other people see things, but now I was seeing things too?

"No! Help me!" Dianne screamed. "It's got me! Help!" Her face was pale and white, and her expression showed nothing but abject horror.

I wondered what to do next, but the house decided for me. Both the Taser and the syringe of insulin suddenly appeared in front of the fireplace. I picked them up and hurried to the front door.

I opened the front door, and three police officers practically fell in. Two ran past me, while the third stayed.

"Are you okay?" the cop asked, taking the weapons from me. "Are you hurt?"

"No," I said. "I think I'm fine." The roots of my hair hurt, and so did the bite on my leg and the scratch marks. The house had a lot to answer for.

When I returned to the living room, one of the cops was handcuffing Dianne, who to my great relief was out of the fireplace and huddled in the corner.

"There's no door! Just walls! Help me! Where am I?" she whimpered pathetically. When she saw me, her demeanour changed at once. "You!" she snarled. "I should've killed you, just like I killed Thomas!" She then let out a string of words that should not be repeated in polite company.

As they dragged her out, something occurred to me. "Who called you?" I asked the third cop.

"Alder Vervain, the private detective, called to say he saw an armed woman approach your house," the police officer said.

I followed them to my front gate and looked up and down the street. Sure enough, there was a familiar car, Alder's car. I thought I could see him, sitting behind the wheel, nothing but a black shadow.

CHAPTER 24

As soon as I returned to the house, I poured myself a glass of wine and ran a hot bath. When I was soaking in the lavender scented bubbles, I called Thyme to fill her in. I wanted her to hear it from me first. The news would be all over town within minutes.

"Would you like to stay with me tonight?" Thyme asked, when I had finished my rundown of the evening's events.

"I'll be fine here, thanks. Is there a safer house in the world?" I went to take another sip, but realised my glass was empty. I had downed the entire glass before I realised that I hadn't eaten for hours. No wonder I felt dizzy.

There was silence for a moment. "Well, you

have a point there," Thyme said. "Why don't you take tomorrow off?"

"Are you kidding me?" I said. "If there's anything I need right now, it's cupcakes."

Thyme laughed. "See you tomorrow then, boss."

"See you tomorrow," I said with a laugh. I carefully set down my empty wine glass, hopped out of the bath, and towelled myself dry.

I went into my bedroom, intending to put on pyjamas and then lie on the sofa and stuff my face with chocolate. At that point, it dawned on me that Camino was likely to come over.

I had not yet worn her gift, a gift that was as thoughtful as it was bizarre. I figured that Camino would come over at some point that night to see how I was doing, once the bush telegraph about the evening's events had reached her, so I carefully pulled on the koala onesie. It was awfully hard to get on, but I finally managed after a struggle. Next, I put on the giant koala slippers.

I looked in the mirror and had a fit of giggles. I looked like an evil monster rather than a nice, fluffy koala. I peered more closely in the mirror. I had deep circles under my eyes and looked haggard. "Well, who wouldn't look tired after the day that

I've had?" I asked the bathroom mirror. Thankfully, it didn't answer.

My eyes fell on the expensive face mask that I'd bought the other day. I read the label. It promised to 'refresh, revitalise, and give the skin a rejuvenated appearance.' That was just what I needed. The ingredients were listed as seaweed, hyaluronic acid, green tea extract, and royal jelly. Sounded good!

I opened the packet and smeared some on my face, carefully avoiding the edges of the koala head-hat. To my dismay, the substance was bright green, lumpy and awfully sticky. Oh well, it felt soothing, and who would see me but Camino? Even she probably wouldn't see me, as the mask was to stay on for only ten minutes.

I wobbled into the kitchen—gee, it was hard to walk in the koala onesie—got a box of chocolates, and went back into the living room.

I picked up the remote and lay on the sofa. Willow and Hawthorn ran into the room, took one look at me, hissed, and ran out, all their fur standing on end.

I laughed, and selected a channel—no, not Mixed Martial Arts. I popped a chocolate in my mouth and flipped the channel to *Love It or List It*, when there was a knock on the door.

"Camino," I said with my mouth full of chocolate truffle. I stood up, and then bent down to retrieve a green glob of face mask that had fallen to the floor. I stuck it back on my face and waddled to the door.

I flung the door open to greet Camino. To my horror, it was not Camino. It was Alder Vervain.

"Argh!" he said, clutching at his throat in shock. He stepped backwards.

"Sorry, it's only me," I said through a mouthful of chocolate. I was aghast. Clearly, Alder wasn't doing much better.

I swallowed the rest of the chocolate whole and then had a coughing fit when it went down the wrong way. I bent over, coughing violently. Tears ran down my cheeks, no doubt making rivulets in the green slime.

When I recovered, I looked back up. To my surprise, Alder was still there. I had half expected he would run away. "I'm wearing a koala onesie and a face mask," I explained.

He nodded. I think he was trying not to laugh. "I can see that."

I felt my face flush, but the green no doubt covered my red cheeks.

"Can I come in? I'd like to talk to you."

"Come in? Into my house?" I said. "Are you feeling okay?"

Alder raised one eyebrow and shot me a strange look. "Err, yes thank you. And you?"

I just shrugged and stood aside. I didn't have the energy to come up with a good reason not to invite him in. I was exhausted. What could I do? I showed him into the living room. "Please have a seat. I'll be right back."

He sat down, and I peered at him. Nothing was happening to him—yet.

"Why are you staring at me?" he asked. "Is something wrong?"

"No reason. No. I'll be right back." I walked as fast as I could to the bathroom and removed the face mask with warm water. I looked in the mirror again once I'd removed the last of the green. My teeth were covered with chocolate. On a brighter note, my skin did look better, but I had no time to be pleased about that now. I waddled to my bedroom and tried to get out of the onesie. The headpiece came off easily, but the rest wouldn't budge. I was just too tired to get it off.

I finally gave up. For all I knew, Alder might be a nervous wreck by now, seeing walls closing in on him, or he might be half way through the fireplace. I had better go and rescue him.

I shuffled into the living room, concerned with what I would see. To my surprise, Alder was as right as rain. Willow was sitting on his lap and Hawthorn was sitting beside him. Both were purring loudly. I sat opposite him, trying not to show my surprise.

"I hope you're all right," Alder said with obvious concern.

"Oh yes," I said, feeling a bit tipsy. "This is the first time I've worn the koala onesie. It was a gift. I didn't buy it. I bought the face mask, though." I stifled the urge to giggle. "I didn't know it was green."

Alder frowned, and then looked at the open wine bottle on the floor next to the remains of the coffee table.

"I've only had one glass of wine," I said defensively, "but I haven't eaten for hours."

"I meant, are you okay after your run in with Dianne Longley? It looks like you had quite a struggle." He gestured to the broken vase and the dead wildflowers strewn everywhere.

"Oh, yes." I waved my hand in dismissal. "I'm okay, though. Thanks for asking. Oh, and thanks for calling the cops."

Alder smiled. "You're welcome. I came tonight because I wanted to see if you were all right, but I also wanted to come clean."

I raised my eyebrows.

"Dianne was the one who hired me to follow you."

I gasped. "She was?"

Alder nodded. "I was suspicious of her right from the beginning. It's obvious to me that she wanted to frame you. I shared this information with the detectives, of course."

"You didn't tell me," I said petulantly.

Alder shrugged. "I couldn't. Client confidentiality and all that."

"I suppose." I narrowed my eyes. He didn't care about client confidentiality when he told the police, but I suppose that was different. But why did the house like him? And why did the cats like him? Camino's divination showed that Alder harboured no ill intent towards me, but that didn't explain why my house and my familiars thought he was so nice. "It's strange that my cats like you," I said. "They're usually not so friendly with strangers."

Alder shrugged. "It makes a nice change. I'm not too popular with some in this town."

"Because of your parents." I clapped my hand over my mouth as soon as I said the words.

Alder did not appear offended, and he did not look surprised. "I'm afraid so," he said. "My parents did alienate a lot of people in town. I myself became estranged from them, in the end."

I thought on that for a moment. "So you don't share your parents' views?"

Alder shook his head. "I don't. Amelia, how much do you know? I mean, obviously Thyme, Camino, Mint and Ruprecht have filled you in to some degree."

"You mean that I'm a witch?" I sure hoped that was what he meant, or this would be yet another embarrassing moment.

To my great relief, Alder nodded. "Yes, but what do you know of your paternal bloodline?"

I was puzzled. "Nothing. I only know that my father was a witch, and his sister, my aunt who left me this house, was a witch, too. Mind you, I didn't have a clue about any of that until I heard about the will. My parents did not once mention anything of the sort. As far as I know, I never met my aunt. Although I think I might've come to this house when I was very young, because I do have vague memories of it."

Alder fidgeted. "There is no such thing as black or white magic. Magic is energy, so what some call black magic, or negative spells, can be turned to good. Magic is magic. It is whether the practitioner uses it for good or bad, that determines whether it is called black or white magic."

My head was spinning. "Why are you telling me this?" Alder looked uncomfortable, and that made me nervous.

Alder stroked Willow, who was looking up at him adoringly. "There are those who are Dark Witches by birth," he continued. "I must explain that this doesn't mean that they are evil. It simply means they have strong power to manifest negative events, until they learn to control it. Hereditary Dark Witches are the most powerful of all witches."

I still wondered why he was telling me this. Although I was somewhat pleased that the magnetic and mysterious Alder Vervain was sitting in my living room, I was tired, somewhat tipsy, dressed in a koala onesie, and had been set upon by a murderer only a short time ago.

Alder looked away from me. "Your aunt learned to control it," he said.

It took some time for the import of his words to

sink in. "My aunt," I said slowly. "My aunt was a Dark Witch? A hereditary Dark Witch?"

Alder nodded.

"My father was a Dark Witch?" I continued.

Alder kept nodding, his expression now impassive.

"And I am…" I could hardly bring myself to say the words. "Are you telling me that I'm a Dark Witch?"

CHAPTER 25

*B*efore he could answer, there was a knock at the door.

"I should be going," Alder said, as he stood up. "I hope I haven't upset you, telling you that. It just means that you're very powerful, and explains why you keep setting things on fire. It's nothing to worry about."

Yet I knew it *was* something to worry about, by the way he said it. Why hadn't the others told me this? They kept telling me I was powerful, but they had never once come straight out and said, "Hey, Amelia, you're a Dark Witch."

I opened the door to see Camino, Thyme, Mint, and Ruprecht standing there. The latter three gasped when they saw me in the onesie, and then all four of them gasped when they saw Alder appear beside me.

"Goodnight, Amelia. Hello, all." He swept passed them with a flourish of his long black coat.

I ushered them inside. They all rounded on me as soon as I shut the door.

"What was he doing here?" Thyme asked.

They were all talking at once. Ruprecht and Mint were both asking me what Alder wanted, while Camino was complimenting me on how much the onesie suited me.

"Into the living room," I said. I hurried ahead of them and then threw myself backwards on the sofa and stretched out. "I'm exhausted. I could sleep for a week." I yawned loudly.

"You need to relax and unwind," Ruprecht said.

"What was Alder doing here?" Thyme asked again.

"He told me that he was working for Dianne— she was the one who'd hired him to watch me. He was pretty sure she was doing it to lay the blame on me, to frame me. He said he told the cops."

"That was nice of him," Thyme said dryly.

I looked up and caught Ruprecht's gaze. At that moment I was fairly sure he knew there was more, but thankfully he didn't say anything.

Mint opened a bag and pulled out some wrapped sandwiches. "We knew you wouldn't get yourself anything to eat, and we were all worried about you."

I was touched.

Soon I was munching on a huge salad sandwich. Willow and Hawthorn were pouncing on my koala slippers. I think Hawthorn was trying to kill them.

"It reminds me of life, in a way," Ruprecht said.

I paused with the sandwich half way to my mouth and stared at him.

He gestured to an old painting of my aunt's, a landscape of water flowing over rocks with a man contemplating the scene from the edge of the creek. The painting was hanging on the wall over an old cedar sideboard. "It's always flowing," he said. "It never stops, in the same way that time flows and never stops. It moves around obstacles, like that rock there, or that branch that fell from the trees above. The point is that water flows, as do our lives. We can't control it, but we can enjoy the highs and forget the lows."

I think I understood. "Since moving here, I haven't had many lows. You've all been great friends to me, and I can't thank you enough."

Ruprecht smiled. "You're a special young woman," he said. "And you'll only grow more special."

My thoughts turned to worry then, as Alder Vervain's words came flooding back to me. I was a Dark Witch, and a hereditary one at that. The most powerful of all witches. Ruprecht and the others had told me I was powerful. They had just never explained to me that the reason I was powerful was because I was a Dark Witch.

Thyme came back into the room with another bottle of wine.

"You know, a river is sort of like life," I said to her.

Thyme laughed. "You've been speaking with Ruprecht."

I chuckled and held out my glass for a refill.

Thyme nodded. "You got it, boss," she said. "On to where the river of life will take us."

I wasn't sure where that would be, whether it would be a well-earned break or yet more excitement. Whatever it was, I was glad that I had my house, my shop, Thyme, and my friends at my side. Even Alder had my back. With them, I could face anything. And I had a feeling that I would.

NEXT BOOK IN THIS SERIES

SIT FOR A SPELL (THE KITCHEN WITCH, BOOK 3)

Sit for a Spell

Amelia Spelled is playing Clue at Camino's house when one of the guests drops dead in the dining room. There was no sign of weapons, so was it Amelia's food? Or something just as unpleasant but more sinister?

The police arrest Camino, so Amelia and her friends are faced with the task of sifting through the suspects.

Will Amelia's attempts to solve the murder be half-baked?

What will Amelia do when she finally discovers Alder's dark secret?

ABOUT MORGANA BEST

Best selling Aussie author, Morgana Best, grew up leaving Tim Tams for the fairies at the bottom of her garden. Now she lives with a half-blind Chocolate Labrador who happily walks into doors, a rescue Dingo who steals zucchinis from the veggie patch, and a cat with no time for nonsense. A former college professor, Morgana enjoys big bowls of pasta, not working out, and visiting the local lighthouse, where she tries to spot the white humpback whale.

www.morganabest.com

Printed in Great Britain
by Amazon